Arion reached into his desk and slid across a small black triangular piece of gleaming plastic.

There were no markings on it. It could've been one of those if-you-had-to-apply-for-it-you-couldn't-afford-it credit cards reserved for multibillionaires she'd read about in a magazine once. Or it could've been a loyalty card for die-hard coffee addicts. Perla had no way of telling. She looked from the card to Arion's face.

"What's that for?" she asked suspiciously.

"That card lets you into that lift. The lift will take you straight to my penthouse. You'll wait for me there—"

"No." Perla stopped what was coming before he could finish.

His nostrils flared. "Excuse me?"

"I won't do...whatever it is you have in mind. I know what you think of me, but you're wrong. What happened between us that night wasn't cheap, and it wasn't tawdry. Not for me, at least. And I despise you for thinking I'd stoop that low to get you to help me—"

"Be quiet for one second and listen." The rough command in his voice dried her words. "You have nowhere to stay. I have a meeting in...exactly eight minutes, which will last for five hours. Minimum. Unless you intend to wander the streets in the rain until I'm finished, my offer is the best you're going to get."

Surprise stamped through her. "Oh, you mean you want me to go up and just...wait for you?" she asked.

"Why, Mrs. Lowell, you sound disappointed."

The Untamable Greeks

Rich, Powerful and Impossible to Resist

Arion, Sakis and Theo Pantelides—three formidable brothers who have risen up from the darkness of their pasts to conquer the world. Powerful, gorgeous and fabulously wealthy, these deliciously arrogant Greeks could have any women they want—but none will ever tame them.

Until now?

What the Greek's Money Can't Buy

April 2014

Sakis is hungry to give in to the forbidden temptation of his buttoned-up PA—but will the cynical Greek pay the price for breaking his golden rule?

What the Greek Can't Resist

June 2014

Perla Lowell is the last woman Arion should want, yet he can't deny himself one night with this irresistible temptress—but what will happen when the dark-hearted Greek discovers the consequences of succumbing to his desire?

Don't miss Theo's story, coming soon!

Maya Blake

—

What the Greek Can't Resist

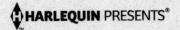

Recycling programs
for this product may
not exist in your area.

ISBN-13: 978-0-373-13729-9

WHAT THE GREEK CAN'T RESIST

First North American Publication 2014

Copyright © 2014 by Maya Blake

HARLEQUIN®
www.Harlequin.com

Printed in U.S.A.

All about the author...
Maya Blake

MAYA BLAKE fell in love with the world of the alpha male and the strong, aspirational heroine when she borrowed her sister's Harlequin® book at age thirteen. Shortly thereafter the dream to plot a happy ending for her own characters was born. Writing for Harlequin® is a dream come true. Maya lives in South East England with her husband and two kids. Reading is an absolute passion, but when she isn't lost in a book she likes to swim, cycle, travel and tweet!

You can get in touch with her via email, at mayablake@ymail.com, or on Twitter, www.twitter.com/mayablake.

Other titles by Maya Blake available in ebook:

WHAT THE GREEK'S MONEY CAN'T BUY
  (The Untamable Greeks)
HIS ULTIMATE PRIZE
MARRIAGE MADE OF SECRETS
THE SINFUL ART OF REVENGE

CHAPTER ONE

THE CAR PARK was as quiet as she'd hoped it would be. Inside her trusted Mini's soothing cocoon, Perla Lowell bit the tip of her pen and searched fruitlessly for the right words.

Four lines. Four paltry lines in two hours were all she'd managed to come up with. She swallowed her despair. Three short days from now she'd have to stand up in front of friends and family and make a speech…

And she had no words.

No, scratch that. She had words. But none rang true. Because the truth… No, she couldn't… *wouldn't* subject anyone to the truth. Her whole life for the past three years had been a colossal lie. Was it any wonder her hands shook every time she tried to write? That her heart pounded with self-loathing for the lies she had to perpetuate for the sake of appearances?

But how could she do anything else? How could she repay kindness with humiliation? Because doing or saying anything else other than what was expected would bring devastation that she couldn't live with.

Anger mingled with despair. With a vicious twist she ripped the paper in two. The cathartic sound echoed through the car and spilled out into the night air. As if loosening the stranglehold she'd exercised on her emotions for longer than she cared to remember, the tears she'd been unable to shed so far now pierced through her tightened chest into her throat.

Her fingers gained a life of their own. Two halves of paper became four, then eight. She ripped again and again, until the sheet spilled through her hands in little wisps of illegible confetti. She upended her hands and watched the mess strewn all over the passenger seat. With a jagged groan, she buried her face in her hands, expecting finally, *finally,* to shed a tear.

The tears never came. They remained locked inside, as they had been for the last two weeks, taunting her, punishing her for daring to wish for them when deep down she knew to cry would be shamefully, deeply disingenuous.

Because, deep inside, she felt…relieved. At a time when she should've been devastated, she felt a shameful lightening of being!

Slowly, she dropped her hands and stared through the windscreen. Her vision cleared and she focused on the palatial Georgian structure in front of her.

Despite its recent multi-million-pound revamp, Macdonald Hall had retained its quintessential old English charm, along with its exclusive membership-by-invitation-only Macdonald Club, and the extensive gold standard golf course that lay beyond the imposing façade.

The centuries-old establishment's only nod to the common man was the cocktail bar, which was open to the public from seven until midnight.

Perla sucked in a deep breath and glanced down at the ripped paper. Guilt bit deep as she acknowledged how good it'd felt to let go. Just this once, to not hold herself back, to not watch her every word or smile when she felt like cursing her fate. To be normal...

The feeling wouldn't last, of course. There was still tomorrow to get through and the next day, and the next.

Dark anguish had her reaching for her bag.

She was far enough away from home not to be recognised here. It was, after all, why she'd driven for over an hour to find a quiet spot to compose the hard-to-find words.

Granted, her journey had been futile so far. But she wasn't ready to return home yet; wasn't ready to face the cloying compassionate gestures and well-meaning, concerned but probing looks.

Her gaze refocused on Macdonald Hall.

One drink. Then she'd drive back home and start again tomorrow.

Opening her bag, she searched for the small brush to run it through her hair in an attempt to tame the unruly curls. When her fingers touched the tube of lipstick, she nearly dismissed it.

Scarlet wasn't really her colour, and normally she wouldn't even glance at one that described itself as *Do Me Red*; she only had the sample lipstick because it'd come free with a book purchase. She would never dare to wear anything so bold. So daring. Even on other women, she found the colour too sensual, too *look-at-my-mouth*.

Fingers trembling, she uncapped the tube, angled the rear-view mirror and carefully applied the lipstick. The unexpected result—the wanton, blatantly sultry image that stared back at her—had her rummaging through her bag for a tissue to reverse the damage. When she came up empty, she paused. Her gaze slowly slid back to the mirror.

Her heart hammered.

Was it so bad? Just for tonight, would it be so bad to look, to *feel* like someone else other than Perla Lowell, *complete fraud*? To forget the pain and unrelenting humiliation she'd suffered for the last three years, if only for a few minutes?

Before she could change her mind, she fumbled for the door handle and stepped out of her car into the cool night air. Her party days might be long behind her but even she knew her simple black sleeveless dress and low black pumps were appropriate for a cocktail bar on a quiet Tuesday night.

And if it wasn't, the worst that could happen was she would be asked to leave. And right now, being thrown out of an exclusive cocktail bar where no one knew who she was would be a walk in the park compared to the monumental farce she had to go through.

A smartly dressed concierge greeted her and directed her through a parquet-floored, oak-panelled hallway to a set of old-fashioned double doors with the words *Bar* fashioned in burnished gold plate above them.

Another similarly dressed man opened the door and tipped his cap to her.

Feeling seriously out of her depth, Perla took fleeting note of the discreetly expensive wood and brocade décor before her eyes zeroed in on the long, low-slung bar. Seriously intimidating rows of drinks were displayed on a revolving carousel and, behind the bar, a bartender twirled a sterling silver set of cocktail shakers while chatting to a young couple.

For a split second, Perla considered turning on her heel and marching straight back out. She forced herself to take a step and another until she reached the unoccupied end of the bar. She'd come this far… Sucking in another sustaining breath, she slid onto the stool and placed her handbag on the counter.

Now what?

'What's a fine girl like you doing in a place like this?'

The cheese-tastic line startled a strained laugh out of her as she turned towards the voice.

'That's better. For a second there, I thought someone had died in here and I hadn't been told,' the bartender's white smile, no doubt tailor-made to drive hormonal girls wild, widened as his gaze traced her face in blatant appraisal. 'You're the second person to walk in here tonight looking like you're a fully paid-up member of the doom-and-gloom brigade.'

In another lifetime, Perla would've found his boyish, perfectly groomed looks charming. Unfortunately, she existed in *this* lifetime, and she'd learnt to her cost that the outside rarely matched the inside.

She willed her smile in place and folded her hands on top of her purse. 'I...I'd like a drink, please.'

'Sure thing.' He leaned in closer and his eyes dropped to her mouth. 'What's your poison?'

Her gaze darted to the cocktails on display. She had no clue what any of them were. The last time she'd been in a bar like this, the drink in fashion had been Amaretto Sour. She wanted to ask for a Cosmopolitan but wasn't even sure if that was still in vogue these days.

She gritted her teeth again and contemplated walking out. Sheer stubbornness made her stay on the stool. She'd been pushed around enough; endured enough. For far too long she'd allowed someone else to call the shots, to dictate the way she lived her life.

No more. Granted, the scarlet lipstick had been a bad idea—it was clear it drew far too much unwanted attention to her mouth—but Perla refused to let that stand in the way of this one small bolstering move.

Squaring her shoulders, she indicated a dark red drink with lots of sunny umbrellas sticking out of it. 'I'll have that one.'

He followed her gaze and frowned. 'The Pomegranate Martini?'

'Yes. What's wrong with it?' she asked when he continued to frown.

'It's a bit…well, lame.'

Her lips firmed. 'I'll take it anyway.'

'Come on, let me—'

'Give the lady what she wants,' a low, dark drawl sounded behind her right shoulder. The smooth but unmistakable cadence in the masculine voice spelled a foreign accent, possibly Mediterranean, that caused a shiver to dance down Perla's spine.

She froze in her seat, her back stiffening as sensation skittered over her skin.

The bartender visibly paled before nodding quickly and sidling off to prepare her cocktail.

Perla felt his silent presence behind her, a palpable force field that bore down and surrounded her with unmistakable power. Her mind shrieked with danger, but for the life of her she couldn't move. Her hand tightened over the strap of her handbag, her fingers plucking frantically at the beads that decorated the dark satin exterior.

'Turn around,' came the low command.

Her back stiffened some more. Another man who wanted to push her buttons. 'Look, I just want to be left alone—'

'Turn around, if you please,' he instructed again in that low, growly voice.

Not *please* but *if you please*. The slightly old-fashioned turn of phrase piqued her curiosity. Coupled with the dark rumble of his voice, Perla was seriously tempted to do as he asked.

But not enough to give in. She remained facing forward.

'I just saved you from becoming the potential target of a chancer with delusions of swagger. The least you can do is turn around and talk to me.'

Despite her stomach flipping again at the impact of his voice, Perla's lips tightened. 'I didn't want nor need your help…and I don't really want to talk to anyone so…'

She glanced towards the bartender with the intention of cancelling her order. The long drive here…the inspired words she'd hoped to write… the idea of a quick drink…the courage-lending scarlet lipstick—probably *that* most of all—had all been an unmitigated disaster. Again she felt pain tighten her chest and fought to keep her emotions under strict control.

Behind her, the man who thought he was her saviour stood in imposing, stifling silence. She knew he was there because his scent lingered in her nostrils—intriguingly spicy, masculine and raw—and she could hear his firm, steady breathing. Again an alien sensation skittered over her skin. The urge to look over her shoulder scythed through her but she refused the urge. She'd failed herself in so many things. Perla refused to fail at this one thing.

Lifting her hand, she tried to catch the bartender's attention but his gaze was focused behind her…on the man whose presence, even without her knowing who he was or her having seen him, spelled power with a capital *P*.

She watched in stunned silence as the bartender nodded in answer to a silent command, rounded the counter with her drink and headed towards a dark corner of the bar.

Outraged, Perla finally turned to find the man—tall, dark-haired and incredibly broad-shouldered—retreating to the table where her drink had been placed along with another, presumably his.

Pure anger spiked through her. Her heels landed on the polished wood floor and she was marching over to him before she fully registered her intention. 'What the hell do you think you're—?'

He turned to face her and the words dried in Perla's throat.

Gorgeous. Astoundingly. Gorgeous. The description lit up like a neon sign in her head— bright, bold, insistent. And so unbelievably real, Perla could only stare in astonishment. Even as she took in the sheer vitality of his olive skin, the lethal bone structure that made up his striking features and the tinge of grey in his hair and designer stubble—her personal, stupidly debilitating weakness—she knew she should never have turned around; never have followed him.

She should've heeded her instinct and walked straight out.

Dear Lord, hadn't she learned from her mistake? She gave a slight shake of her head and tried to step back. She had no business being here; no business staring at a man the way she was staring at this stranger. If anyone found out...

Move!

Her feet wouldn't comply.

Deep hazel eyes bored into hers, then slowly traced her body from head to toe and back again. Perla found herself holding her breath, her fingers once again working frantically over the beads on her handbag.

The breathtaking stranger's gaze paused at her

hair. 'Is that colour real?' he rasped in that knee-weakening, pulse-stroking voice.

'Excuse me?'

'That shade of red. Is it real?' he demanded.

A little bit of her entrancement receded. 'Of course it's real. Why would I dye—?' She stopped as it occurred to her then that he didn't know her and therefore wouldn't know that the last thing she concerned herself with was vanity in the form of artificial hair colour. There was no one to please or pander to and she was too busy surviving to think about frivolous things such as what colour to dye her hair. 'It's real, okay? Now will you explain what you're playing at? That's my drink you've just commandeered.'

'Your manners seemed to have deserted you. I'm merely redressing the situation.' He pulled out a chair. 'Please sit down.'

Lifting an eyebrow, she remained standing.

With a shrug, he remained standing too.

She blew out an irritated breath. 'My manners haven't deserted me. You stepped in and took over a situation I had under control. What did you think, that the bartender would've vaulted over the counter and assaulted me in plain sight of the other customers?' she snapped.

He broke his fascination with her hair and dropped his gaze to capture hers. 'What other customers?' he asked.

'The couple over there—' She broke off as

she looked around. The young couple were gone. Aside from a waiter who was clearing a few other tables, only the tall stranger and bartender remained in the bar. As she watched, the waiter walked through a set of swinging doors and disappeared.

She swallowed. 'This is a reputable place. Things like that don't happen here.'

'And what exactly do you base that statistic on? Are you a frequent visitor?'

She flushed. 'No, of course not. And I'm not naïve. I just…I just think—'

'That predators in Savile Row suits are less vicious than those in hoodies?' His smile didn't reach his eyes.

'No, that's not what I meant. I came here for a quiet drink.' Her gaze dropped to the bold and garish-looking cocktail standing next to his dark-coloured spirit.

This was fast getting out of hand, and she needed to think about getting back. Or she would have more explaining to do.

He indicated the chair one more time. 'You can still have it. And you needn't worry about making conversation. We can sit here and not… talk.'

His words piqued her curiosity. Or maybe she just wanted a distraction from the pain and chaos that awaited her the moment she left this place.

She forced herself to look at him—really look past the surface hurt-your-eyes gorgeousness of the man—past the powerful shoulders underneath the impeccable suit and loosened silk tie. His hair was slightly ruffled, as if he'd shoved a hand through it once or twice.

The brackets around his mouth were deeply grooved and when she chanced another look into his eyes, what Perla glimpsed made her heart hammer.

In that instant she knew he wasn't here to prey on unsuspecting or vulnerable women. That wasn't to say women would be safe from the sensual aura and sheer charisma that oozed from him. Far from it.

But for tonight, in this very moment, whoever this man was, the emotions lurking in his eyes weren't of a predatory nature. The pain she saw resonated with her on so deep a level, she found it hard to breathe through it.

His eyes narrowed, as if sensing the direction of her thoughts. He stiffened and his mouth firmed. For a moment she thought he was going to change his mind about his earlier invitation.

Abruptly he moved a step forward, touched the back of the chair. 'Sit down. Please,' he repeated.

Perla sat. In silence, he pushed her drink towards her.

'Thank you,' she murmured.

He inclined his head and raised his glass towards her. 'To not talking.'

She touched her glass to his; a surreal feeling overtook her as she stared at him over the rim of her glass and took a sip of her cocktail. The potent alcohol hit the back of her throat, warming and cooling at the same time. The tartness of the pomegranate burst on her tongue, making her close her eyes in a single moment of pleasure before the strength of his scrutiny propelled her eyelids back open.

Once again, he seemed fascinated with her hair. It took every ounce of self-control she possessed not to fiddle with it. She sucked harder on her straw, partly to finish the drink quicker so she could leave and partly because it gave her something to do other than stare at this hauntingly beautiful man.

They sipped their drinks in silence.

With a very unsettling amount of regret, Perla set her empty glass down.

The stranger followed suit. 'Thank you.'

'For what?'

'For controlling the urge to indulge in idle chit-chat.'

'I told you, that's not what I came here for. If it was, I'd have brought a friend. Or come earlier when I knew there would be more people here. I presume you chose this time for the same reason.'

A shaft of pain flitted over his features but was gone in the next instant. 'You presume correct.'

She shrugged. 'Then there's no need to thank me.'

He stilled, the only movement his gaze as it flew once again to her hair. When it traced down to her mouth, Perla became very much aware of the scarlet lipstick. Before she could stop herself, she licked her tingling lower lip.

His low hiss was an alien sound that sent a fresh wave of goose bumps over her skin. She'd never elicited such a reaction in a man before. Perla wasn't sure whether to be pleased or terrified.

'Are you staying here, at Macdonald Hall?' she asked, in the hope of deflecting the unsettling feeling his hiss had elicited.

The stranger's hand tightened slowly into a fist on the table. 'For tonight and the next few nights, yes.'

She looked from his hand to his face. 'Why do I get the feeling that you don't want to be here?' she asked.

'Because we don't always get to decide our own fate. But I'm obliged to be here for the next few days. It doesn't mean I'm pleased about it.'

She glanced at his empty glass. 'Then I suppose you'll be upgrading to a bottle instead of a glass shortly?'

He shrugged. 'Drinking is one way of making the time pass faster, I suppose.'

Danger crawled across her skin, sparking a flame in her belly, but Perla couldn't move. 'When you're alone in a bar at almost midnight, I don't really see much else to entertain you.' Her voice emerged huskier than she'd ever heard it.

He raised a dark eyebrow. 'But I'm not alone. Not any more. I've saved you, a damsel in distress, and my reward is your company for now.'

'I'm not a damsel in distress. Besides, you don't know me from a blade of grass. I could be one of those predators you described, for all you know, Mr...?'

Her blatant demand for his name went unanswered as he nodded to the bartender and indicated their empty glasses.

'I don't think I should have another drink—'

Hooded hazel eyes trapped hers. 'But we're just getting to know one another. You were telling me about being a ruthless predator.'

'And you wanted to be alone less than ten minutes ago, remember? Besides, what makes you think I want to get to know you?'

His small smile was both self-assured and self-pitying, a curious, intriguing combination. 'I don't. Forgive me for the assumption. If you wish you leave, you may do so.'

Again the courteous words laced with arrogance set her teeth on edge. But Perla found she couldn't look away from the fascinating man, whose extremely powerful aura held a wealth of pain and sadness that drew her…made her hesitate.

She licked her lips and immediately regretted it when his gaze latched onto the movement. 'I don't need your permission but I…I'll stay for another drink.'

He nodded solemnly. '*Efharisto.*' The way his voice and sensual lips formed the word made her stomach perform an annoying little flip.

'What does that mean?'

'Greek, for *thank you.*'

'Oh, you're Greek? I love Greece. I visited Santorini a long time ago for the wedding of a client. I remember thinking at the time it's where I'd like to get married one day. That has got to rank up there as one of the most beautiful places on earth—' Perla drew to a sharp halt as his face tightened suddenly. 'I'm sorry. Mindless chit-chat?'

One corner of his mouth lifted. 'It's not as mindless as I thought it would be. So you love Greece. What else do you love?'

Her gaze dropped to the table, then immediately rose to meet his, almost against her will. 'Is this the part where I say long walks in the rain with that special someone?'

'Only if it's true. Personally, I detest the rain. I prefer wall-to-wall sunshine. And the sea.'

'And the special someone is optional?'

That look she'd caught on his face earlier returned—the cross between ragged pain and guilt—and this time it stayed for several moments before he shrugged.

'If you're lucky enough to have the choice, and to hang onto your good fortune.'

She bit her lip but was stopped from answering as the bartender delivered their order. Again silence ensued as they sipped their drinks. Only this time, when his gaze travelled over her, she boldly watched him back.

The silvery strands that blended into his temples coupled with the designer stubble gave him a seriously gorgeous but distinctly imposing look that sent her heart thudding faster. He looked vaguely familiar. Mentally shrugging, Perla concluded she must have seen him in the newspaper or on TV. His air of importance and easy way he commanded power lent itself to that theory. And, of course, he was here, at Macdonald Hall, one of the most exclusive private sport clubs in the country.

His fingers curled around his glass and she watched him lift his drink to his lips, his gaze staying on hers. Heat rushed through her, filling her up in places she'd begun to think were frozen forever. Perla tried to tell herself it was the alcohol but in an angry rush of rejection she forced herself to face the truth. She was done lying to herself, to glossing over the bare truth in order to lessen her pain.

No more!

She was attracted to this man. To his gorgeous, pain-etched face, the haunted hazel eyes, the strong stubbled jaw she wanted to run her fingers over just to see if it felt as rough as his manly, callused fingers. The mental pictures reeling through her head should've shocked and shamed her. But, for tonight, Perla was determined to suspend shame. And really, when had looking been a crime? And he was as exquisite a specimen as any.

'Be careful, little one. This big, bad wolf has vicious, merciless teeth.'

The softly voiced caution ripped her from her thoughts.

What was she doing?

In a rush, she put down her barely touched drink, stood up and snatched her handbag. 'I… you're right. Caution is usually my middle name so, um…thanks for the drink.' Her tongue felt thick with the lack of knowledge of the proper etiquette. 'And for the company.'

Her breath caught when he stood to tower over her. 'Did you drive here?' he demanded.

'Yes, but I barely touched my second drink and—'

'My driver will deliver you home.'

A mixture of fear and anxiety roiled through her. Imagine the gossip if she returned home in a strange man's car! Granted it was almost midnight but it would only take one sighting for the rumour mill to spin into overdrive. She had enough on her plate to deal with as it was.

'No. That's very kind of you but it's not necessary.'

His striking, very hypnotic eyes narrowed. In that moment, all Perla noticed were his insanely thick eyelashes and the way his mouth turned down when he was displeased. The urge to take that look from his face shocked her into stepping back. When she took another step back, he followed.

'Let me at least walk you to your car.'

'I'm perfectly capable—'

'That wasn't a suggestion.'

'Didn't you warn me about Savile-Row-dressed predators a short while ago?'

That sad, almost haunted smile made another appearance. Those endlessly fascinating fingers delved into his bespoke jacket and emerged with his smartphone. He tapped the three-digit emergency number into it and extended it to her, pointing to the dial button. 'Hit that button if I so much as exhale the wrong way between here and your car. But make no mistake, I'm walking you out of here and seeing you into your car.'

With a shaky hand, she took his phone. His fingers brushed then stilled against hers. Warmth infused her. Without thinking, she rubbed her fingers against his and heard his sharp intake of breath as he fell into step beside her.

The walk to her car took minutes but it felt like the longest walk of her life. Beside her, the tall, dark and dangerous stranger lessened his significantly long stride to match hers. Over and over again, Perla felt the heat of his gaze travel over her. She forced herself not to glance at him. To do so would've wavered her intent, made her give in to the intensely mortifying need that had taken root inside her.

But, with each dreaded step to her car, Perla felt as if she was fighting a losing battle. What had she achieved by coming here? So far, a big fat *nothing*. She hadn't even broached the task she would give everything not to have to deal with. A task she would've given everything not to return to.

Surely it wasn't wrong to make this moment with this perfect stranger last a little longer? She gave an inward sigh.

Who was she kidding? Fate had stuck two fingers up to her over and over. Why should tonight be any different?

She stopped beside her car and turned towards him. With a deep breath, she held out his phone. 'I told you this wasn't necessary. But again, thanks.'

He barely glanced at the gadget. 'You're not out of danger yet.'

She looked up into his face. 'What do you mean?' she asked, her voice a touch too breathless.

He stepped closer, his body heat slamming into her, making her head spin. 'Hang onto it for a little while longer. I don't want to end our conversation, not just yet.'

Perla's pulse rate shot up even higher. 'Why?'

'Because...' He seemed to catch himself just then. A frown creased his brow and he shook his head.

When he stepped back, a spasm of fear that she was losing him made her lean towards him. 'Because...?'

He focused on her. Hazel eyes pinned her to the spot, then rushed to her hair, over her face, her neck, down to her toes before coming back to her face. He muttered something under his breath, something in his native tongue that held no meaning for her.

'Tell me your name.'

Her mouth dried. 'It's...Pearl.' She cringed inwardly at the small fib but, growing up, her unusual name had often been mistaken for the more common *Pearl*. Besides, the anonymity made her feel less exposed.

His hooded gaze dropped to her lips, its message so blatantly sexual, her breath stalled in her chest. 'I have an irresistible urge to kiss you, Pearl. Does that make you want to run?'

The rawness behind the words rocked her to her soul, resonated beside her own turmoil. She watched his eyes slowly grow darker, more tormented. Before she could consciously stop herself, she reached up and cupped his taut cheek.

'No. But it makes me want to know what's wrong,' she said softly.

He made a rough sound under his breath, like a proud but wounded animal. 'Nothing I wish to bore you with tonight.'

'What makes you think I'll be bored? Perhaps I need the distraction as much as you do,' she said in a rush of confession. She swayed closer and stopped herself a mere whisper from him. 'Perhaps I want to give you what you want because it's what I want too?' It felt a little absurd, having this conversation with him. But it also felt… oddly right.

'Be very careful what you wish for, little one,' he breathed.

'Oh, but I have been. Very careful. Too careful at times. I'm tired of being careful.'

His hand reached up to cover hers, pressed her hand harder into his jaw. Underneath her fingers, his stubble bristled against her palm, sparking an electric current that transmitted up her arm and suffused her whole body.

'Don't offer temptation you won't be able to deliver on,' he warned.

'Are you challenging me?'

'I'm offering a word of caution. I don't wish to frighten you so perhaps you should leave now,' he grated out. 'Or stay, if you're brave enough. I accept that the choice is yours. But decide quickly.'

Contrary to his words, his fingers caught and

imprisoned a thick strand of her hair, his movement almost reflexive as he passed the tresses through his fingers repeatedly.

Caught in a sensation so alien and yet so right, Perla closed that last tiny gap between them. Strong hands immediately caught her to him. She collided with over six feet of lean muscle that knocked the air out of her lungs.

Before she could draw breath, his lips settled over hers. Every thought flew out of her head as she became lost in pure, electric sensation. He kissed her as if she was life-giving oxygen, as if he needed her to survive. That knowledge more than anything caught a fragile spot inside her; shook it free and allowed her to enjoy this, to become a part of this small healing process that they both needed.

With a groan, she pressed herself closer until she could feel his heartbeat against her breasts, the ridged chest muscles crushing her softer ones. Both his hands encompassed her waist and lifted her up onto the bonnet of her car. Then he plunged both fingers into her hair, angled her face up to his and proceeded to dive deeper into their kiss.

Only the need for air finally separated them.

Perla's breaths puffed out into the cool night and threatened to cease altogether when she saw the smear of scarlet on his lips.

Reaching up, she touched his mouth. He made

a sound of mingled pain and pleasure and she almost lost her mind.

'I…I…' She wasn't sure exactly what she wanted to say. Only that she needed to make sense of what was happening to her. 'Is that enough?' From the depths of her soul came a yearning for him to say no.

When he shook his head, her heart soared.

'No, it's not. The taste of you is intoxicating. I want to drown in you.' He captured her face in his hands and kissed her some more, murmuring phrases in Greek she had no hope of understanding. When he released her, he was breathing hard. Pulling her close, he rested his forehead against hers. '*Theos*…this is madness, but I can't let you go. Not yet.' He pulled back and tilted her face to his, his hazel eyes swirling with the same potent need that twisted inside her. 'Stay with me tonight, Pearl.'

Her decision was instant; so frighteningly committed that she forced herself to remain silent when she wanted to blurt it out. Her fingers moved again over his soft, sensual lips. He captured them and kissed her knuckle. It occurred to her that she held his phone in her other hand. One small movement of her thumb and this would be over—decision made.

Or she could give the answer she wanted, no, *needed* to give. Take back a small piece of herself before she had to face the world again.

'I don't even know your name,' she ventured.

'My name is Arion. If it pleases you, you can call me Ari.'

She shook her head. 'It pleases me to call you Arion.'

She loved the way her lips curled around his name. So much so, she said it again. 'Arion…'

His eyes darkened. 'You like my name?' he rasped.

'I *love* your name. I've never heard it before… Arion.' She couldn't resist the temptation to try it out one more time.

He caught her up to him and banded one arm around her waist. His laser-like gaze scoured her face as if he was trying to read her innermost thoughts. 'The way you say my name… You are dangerous, Pearl *mou*.'

Laughter, long suppressed under the pain of just *existing*, scratched from her throat. 'Wow… I'm *dangerous*? That's a first.'

'What have other men called you?'

The question sobered her up. Familiar humiliation threatened to crawl over her but she determinedly pushed it away. Tonight was *her* night, *her* choice. She refused to let thoughts of past failures intrude.

'What do you think they've called me?'

'Breathtaking. Stunning. A beauty Aphrodite herself would be jealous of,' he breathed against her neck as his lips caressed her skin. 'Your hair is incredible, the colour of a Greek sunset.'

Perla's breath hitched in her lungs. Unbidden, tears sprang into her eyes. Blinking wildly before he spotted them, she forced herself not to be drawn in by the seductive words.

'Am I close?' He lifted his head and rubbed his stubble—as rough as she'd imagined it would be—against her cheek.

Liquid heat melted her insides.

'Not even a little. But don't let that stop you.'

'Beautiful Pearl, I want to see your hair spread over my pillow. I want to bury myself in it, strangle myself with it.' The hoarse litany made her draw back and stare at him. Once again, his face was stamped in pain. But, alongside it, desire, strong and unmistakable, burned right into her soul. 'Does that frighten you?'

'I want to say no, but I am a little frightened, yes. I've never done this before but I want to. Very much.' So badly she couldn't think straight. The need to forget, just for a short while, what faced her in the next few days, was so strong she couldn't breathe for the need of it. 'Right now, I'm so desperate for you I don't know how long I can stand it.'

'Then stay. I will give you everything you desire.' About to kiss her again, he suddenly froze. 'Unless you're not free to be with me?'

'What do you mean?'

'Is there a lover or a husband?' came the tight, throaty demand.

The arrow of guilt that lanced through her made her freeze too.

This is your night. Yours! Tomorrow will come soon enough.

'I'm free to be with you, Arion. I'll stay with you tonight if you want me to.'

His suite was *probably* the last word in luxury; the fixtures and fittings ones she'd *probably* have ogled if she'd had a chance to take even a single note.

But with Arion's mouth on hers, his fingers in her hair and his body pressed close and hot against hers, Perla didn't notice one single thing about the third-floor suite, except that the *RS* button he'd pressed in the lift stood for Royal Suite.

She did notice the large red velvet sofa he laid her down on the minute they entered his suite's pitch-sized living room. Although the memory of it disappeared once he'd shrugged off his jacket and tie and freed his shirt from his trousers.

His chest once he unbuttoned his shirt instantly made her mouth dry, then flood with longing as she stared at hard contours and smooth bronzed muscles. Hairless and divine, his stunning beauty made need she'd never known pulse through her.

But that was a fraction of what she felt when he dropped his trousers and stepped out of his cot-

ton boxers. His erection stood strong and proud…
and big.

Just then, the enormity of what she was doing
hit her between the eyes.

She was about to lose her virginity to a complete stranger.

CHAPTER TWO

A DEEP SHUDDER ripped through Perla and she barely stopped her teeth from chattering like a wooden marionette in a child's hand.

The sound she made as Arion, the man she had no knowledge of a mere hour ago, came towards her made him pause and frown.

'Are you cold?' he asked.

She was anything but. She shook her head, forcing a laugh. 'No. I'm a little nervous. I haven't—' She stopped. What was the use of telling him of her inexperience? Whether she pleased or disappointed him, she'd never set eyes on this gorgeous man again. They were using each other to forget their pain, to hold the darkness at bay. This wasn't the time to spill innermost secrets. It was the time to forget they existed. 'It's nothing.'

He nodded as if he understood. Then he took a single step forward, and angled himself over her. 'I'll make it good. I promise,' he vowed, and she forgot everything else.

The kiss was hotter, deeper than the one he'd

delivered at the car. This time his tongue probed her mouth with a sensual force that spoke of his need. Fists clamped in her hair, he went even deeper, his groan of satisfaction echoing her own as her fingers sought and found firm, heated, *naked* shoulders.

His skin felt like pure heaven. Velvety smooth and oh so gloriously luxuriant, she explored him from shoulder to back, then lower. When she moulded her hands over his bare bottom, then dug her nails into his taut flesh, he wrenched his lips from hers with a tortured groan. His breath came out in pants as he stared down at her, eyes dark with lust.

'Promise me you'll do that when I'm deep inside you.'

Heat drenched her from head to toe. From somewhere she summoned the strength to speak. 'I promise.'

He licked the corner of her mouth in a move so simple and yet so powerfully erotic, she felt as if her insides would combust. She gave a heartfelt groan when he pushed himself off her. 'For that to happen, *glikia mou*, you need to be as naked as I am.'

Perla stared down at herself, stunned that the power of his lust hadn't melted the clothes off her. When he grabbed her arms and pulled her up, she went willingly. The slide of her zip was loud and intrusive in the silent room. Unwanted thoughts once again threatened to ruin the moment. *What the hell are you doing? Leave. Leave now!*

As if he could tell, he quickened his movements. Within seconds, he was bending over her once more, his mouth trailing down her neck, washing away her doubt, re-igniting the flames that had merely been banked.

'Tell me how you like it, Pearl *mou*,' he rasped against the valley between her breasts. 'Tell me your favourite position and I'll do it to you.'

Panic momentarily seized her. She searched her mind for terms she'd heard of. 'Doggie style,' she blurted, then cringed as her face flamed.

Thank God he didn't notice. For some strange reason, he seemed as fascinated with her breasts as he'd been with her hair. Moulding them in his hands, he licked first one hardened nipple, then the other, then pulled them simultaneously into his mouth. At her deep groan, he smiled.

'That is one of my favourite positions too,' he said. His teeth grazed over her nipples, then he trailed kisses lower…lower, until she realised his destination.

He ignored the staying hand she put on his shoulder.

'No…'

'*Yes!*' With a hot look from darkened eyes, he parted her thighs.

She held her breath but, at the first sweep of his tongue, she exhaled as pleasure she'd never known rushed over her. Before she could react to that first wave, he began a series of flicks that made stars dance before her eyes. Expertly, he pleasured her, relentless in his need to make her lose control. Buffeted by sensations she'd never experienced, Perla fought both the urge to withdraw from that wicked tongue and press her hips closer. Her head thrashed on the cushion as an unfamiliar sensation pushed her towards a blissful peak.

'Arion! Oh, God… Oh!' She let out a scream as her climax broke over her. Jerking uncontrollably, she sobbed as pleasure washed over her and sucked her under. When he gathered her in his arms and pulled her into his body, Perla sobbed harder.

Through it all he murmured soft words of praise and comfort, a balm her soul desperately needed. An eternity later, he started to pull away. Her protesting mutter was met with another kiss.

'Patience, *pethi mou*, now the real fun begins,' he said with dark promise.

Slowly, Perla rubbed the tears from her eyes.

Opening her eyes, she found him kneeling on the sofa, sliding on a condom. The sight of him, large and powerful and ready, sent another pulse of lust through her.

When he probed her entrance, Perla felt a moment's twinge, a shaky feeling of disconnect. It faded away the moment he pressed himself deeper. At her body's further resistance, he paused with a groan.

'You're not ready. I'm sorry, I was a little impatient.'

She slid her hands through his hair and barely resisted raising her head to kiss him. 'I want you.'

He gave another groan and kissed her. 'You're not ready and I don't want to hurt you.'

Mistaking his meaning, Perla spread her thighs wider and ventured her hips closer. 'I'm ready now.'

Arion raised his head, a slightly puzzled look crossing his face. 'Pearl—'

'Please, don't keep us waiting.' Emboldened by his groan, she pressed even closer. He slid in another delicious inch.

The discomfort grew as he pushed in but the rush, the pleasure that followed behind it was so much worth the momentary pain. Perla's breath fractured as she sighed in bliss. Arion's grip tightened in her hair with the full surge of his body.

'*Theos!* You're so tight. So gorgeous.' The warmth of his breath washed over her neck a second before his lips found and captured hers. His tongue slid into her mouth, its movement as bold and as raw as his full, relentless thrusts.

Bliss washed over her so completely, Perla had no idea where sensation started and ended. Clamping her legs around his waist, she took him fully into her body. Pleasure crested in giant waves over her. But, just as she prepared to give herself over to it, he pulled out of her. Rising to his feet, he tugged her off the sofa and onto the floor.

'On your knees,' he commanded. 'It's time to give you what you want.'

Her heart hammering with excitement, Perla complied. He came up behind her, bent her over the seat and entered her from behind.

'Oh, my God!' The cry was ripped from her soul, pleasure so profound radiating from inside her she thought she'd pass out.

Arion's fingers slid through her hair over and over as he thrust inside her. Perla had never thought of her hair as an erogenous area. In fact, up till that moment, she'd never thought pleasure like this was possible.

Dear heaven, how wrong she'd been. She screamed as he pounded into her, his hoarse voice reciting her name over and over. Once again the precipice approached, the stars beckoning with a radiance she knew would touch her for ever. Behind her, Arion slid back and rested on his knees. Firm hands urged her back, all the while continuing the relentless pace that stalled her breath.

'Ride me,' he encouraged, his deep voice raw and urgent.

Spreading her legs wider, Perla eased herself back, the change in pace escalating her pleasure even higher. Hands gripping the sofa to steady herself, she rode herself to ecstasy. Her breath choked on a scream as her orgasm hit her. One hand clamped around her middle, Arion eased another hand over her belly to tease her clitoris, prolonging her climax. The wave seemed endless; he continued to thrust inside her despite her pleas for mercy. Just when she thought she'd expire from pleasure, she heard his deep groan. He buried his face in her hair, his thrusts growing uneven as pleasure spasms gripped him.

Several minutes later, he planted kisses on her neck and shoulder, one hand still gripped on her waist. 'I can't decide whether you're an angel or a witch, sent to torment me or bring me heaven.'

Her breath caught on a soft blissful sigh. 'Can I be both?'

'With hair like that, you can be anything you want.'

She managed to lift her head to glance over her shoulder at him. 'You have a freaky fascination with my hair.'

'A fascination which includes seeing it spread over my pillow.' He pulled out of her with a dark groan, scooped her into his arms and headed down a short hallway.

Once again she barely registered her surroundings. But, even while he secured another condom, Arion's gaze held her captive, the look he sent her exciting her in ways she'd never have dreamt was possible. When he took command of her body once more, Perla gave herself over into his arms, a willing slave for the pleasures in store…

She woke with a start, then fought to regulate her breathing so as not to wake the sleeping man beside her.

A sneak peek at the bedside clock showed it was half past two in the morning.

Perla glanced at Arion—goodness, she didn't even know his surname. Well, he didn't know her real name, which was a blessing in disguise, she supposed. Not that their paths would cross again in a million years.

Her gaze devoured his sleeping form. God, he was truly spectacular, and the pleasures he'd shown her would remain unforgettable. Watching the steady rise and fall of his massive chest, she felt her nipples peak again as excitement crawled over her.

She bit her lip and forced herself to get up. She dressed in silence, holding her breath every time he moved. The small part of her that hoped he would wake and stop her leaving was ruthlessly squashed.

They could never be more than ships passing in the night. She carried too much baggage and, from what she'd glimpsed in his eyes, he carried a shipload of his own baggage. All the same, her fingers slowed on her zip. Maybe it didn't have to be this way, maybe she could…

Stay? Dear Lord, what was she thinking?

Doing anything of that sort was totally out of the question. She had *no* choice but to leave.

If for no other reason than the fact that between now and Friday morning when she had to stand before a congregation and speak, she had her dead husband's eulogy to write.

CHAPTER THREE

THE SMALL CHAPEL was packed to the rafters. Outside, a clutch of news vans and reporters were stationed, poised and ready for the opportunity to snap any picture that would feed the media frenzy of the notoriety behind this funeral.

So far, Perla hadn't found the courage to turn around to see just how many people had wedged themselves into the tiny chapel. The one glance as people had filed in had been enough to terrify her. But she hadn't missed the trio of limousines that had crawled past and parked ominously on the chapel lawn.

Morgan's bosses. Probably Sakis Pantelides and various executives from Pantelides Shipping Inc. The letter announcing their attendance had arrived yesterday.

She supposed she should be thankful they were bothering to attend, considering the nefarious circumstances leading to Morgan's death. A small, bitter part of her wished they hadn't bothered. Their presence here would, no doubt, keep up the media frenzy, and she also couldn't dismiss the fact that she'd had to keep demanding information from Pantelides Inc. before she'd been given very brief details of what had happened to her husband.

Granted, Sakis Pantelides had been gentle and infinitely considerate when he'd broken the horrific news to her but the fact remained that Morgan Lowell, the man she'd married, and whose secret she'd kept—*still kept*—had died under suspicious circumstances in a foreign country after trying to get away with defrauding his employer. Pantelides Inc. had kept a lid on the fact to protect itself from adverse publicity.

What no one realised was that *this* was yet another morsel of unwanted truth she had to keep to herself; another detail she couldn't share with Morgan's parents, who had idolised their son and remained devastated by his death. She'd been forced to gloss over the truth for their sake. Again…

She clenched her hands and forced herself to focus. She had more important things to think about now, like how she could stand up and speak of her husband when another man's face, the fevered recollection of another man's hands and the thrust of his hard body repeatedly flashed through her brain.

Dear God, what had she done? What had she been thinking?

Although guilt clawed through her belly, the

shame she expected to feel remained way below an acceptable level. In fact she barely felt anything except the forceful presence of her one-night lover, deep inside her, surrounding her, pulsing around her like a live electric current with every breath she took.

She'd taken three showers this morning, all in the vain hope of washing herself free of his scent. But it was as if he'd invaded her thoughts as well as her pores. Behind her, whispered voices surged higher and she heard shuffling as the congregation made way for new arrivals.

Perla's breath stalled as she caught the familiar scent again. She bit her lip and closed her eyes. *God, please give me strength because I'm seriously losing it here.*

When her elderly neighbour and only friend Mrs Clinton's hand covered hers, she gratefully clutched it. The discerning woman had wisely put herself between Perla and Morgan's parents but she felt their heartbreak with every fibre of her being.

For their sake, for the kindness and open warmth they'd shown her, she had to keep it together. They were the reason she'd borne this humiliation for so long. Morgan had known that. Had banked on it, in fact, and used it as the perfect blackmail tool when she'd threatened to leave him—

'Not long before it starts. Don't worry, dear; in

less than an hour, it'll be over. I went through the same thing with my Harry,' she whispered. 'Everyone means well, but they don't know the best they can do in times like these is to leave you alone, do they?'

Perla attempted a response and only managed a garbled croak. Mrs Clinton patted her hand again reassuringly. With relief, she heard the organ starting up. As she stood, Perla caught the scent again, and quickly locked her knees as she swayed.

She glanced to the side and saw a tall, imposing man with a thin scar above his right eye standing next to a striking blonde.

Sakis Pantelides, the man who'd phoned two weeks ago with news of her husband's death. His condolences had been genuine enough but after her discovery of just what Morgan had done to his company, Perla wasn't so sure his attendance here was an offer of support.

Her gaze shifted to the proprietorial arm he kept around the woman, his fiancée, Brianna Moneypenny, and she felt a twinge of shame-laced jealousy.

He caught her gaze and he gave a short nod in greeting before returning his attention to the front.

She faced forward again, but the unsettling feeling that had gripped her nape escalated. The feeling grew as the ceremony progressed. By the time the priest announced the eulogy reading, Perla's stomach churned with sick nerves. She pushed it away. Whatever emotional turmoil she was experiencing had nothing to do with the Pantelides family and everything to do with what she'd done on Tuesday night. And those memories had no place here in this chapel, today.

No matter what Morgan had put her through, she had to do this without breaking down. She had to endure this for his parents' sake.

They'd offered her the only home she'd ever known, and the warmth she'd only ever dreamed about as a child.

Another pat from Mrs Clinton gave her the strength to keep upright. She thought she heard a sharp intake of breath behind her but Perla didn't turn around. She needed every ounce of focus to stride past the coffin holding her dead husband... the husband who, while he'd been alive, had taken great pleasure in humiliating her; the husband who even in death...seemed to be mocking her.

She got to the lectern and unfolded the piece of paper. Nerves gripped her and, although she knew it was rude, she couldn't look up from the sheet. She had a feeling she would lose her nerve if her gaze strayed from the paper in her hand.

Clearing her throat, she moved closer to the microphone.

'I met Morgan at the uni bar on my first day on campus. I was the wide-eyed, clueless outsider who had no clue what went into a half-fat, double-shot pumpkin spice latte—except maybe the pumpkin—and he was the second-year city dude every girl wanted to date. Even though he didn't ask me out until I was in my last year, I think I fell in love with him at first sight…'

Perla carried on reading, refusing to dwell on how overwhelmingly wrong she'd been about the man she'd married; how utterly gullible she must have been to have had the wool pulled over her eyes so effectively until it was too late.

But now was not the time to think of past mistakes. She read on, saying the *right* thing, *honouring* the man who right from the very beginning of their marriage had had no intention of honouring *her*.

'…I'll always remember Morgan with a pint in his hand and a twinkle in his eye, telling rude jokes in the uni bar. *That* was the man I fell in love with and he'll always remain in my heart.'

Unshed tears clogged her throat again. Swallowing, she folded the sheet and finally gathered the courage to look up.

'Thank you all for coming—'

She choked to a halt as her gaze clashed with a pair of sinful, painfully familiar hazel eyes.

No.

Oh, God, no…

Her knees gave way. Frantically, she clutched at the lectern. She felt her hand begin to slip. Someone shouted and moved towards her. Unable to breathe or halt her crumpling legs, she cried out.

Several people rushed towards her. Hands grabbed her before she fell, righted her, helped her down from the dais.

And, through it all, Arion Pantelides stared at her from where he stood next to the man she'd guessed was Sakis Pantelides, icy condemnation blazing from his eyes and washing over her until her whole body went numb.

Ari tried to breathe past the vice squeezing his chest, past the thick anger and acrid bitterness lashing his insides. The pain that rose alongside it, he refused to acknowledge.

Why would he feel pain? He had no one to blame but himself. After all life had thrown at him, he'd dared to believe he could reach out and seek goodness when there was none to be had. Only disappointment. Only heartache. Only disgust.

But still the anger came, thick and fast and strong, as he stared at Pearl...no, *Perla* Lowell, the woman who'd lied about her name and slithered into his bed while her husband's body was barely cold.

Disgust roiled through him. Even now, the memory of what they'd done to each other made fiery desire pool in his groin. Gritting his teeth, he forced his fists to unclench as he stamped down on the emotion.

He'd let himself down, spectacularly and utterly.

On the most sacred of days, when he should've been honouring his past, he'd allowed himself to succumb to temptation.

Temptation with absolutely the wrong woman.

One who'd turned out to be as duplicitous and as sullied as the husband she was burying.

'Do you know what's going on with her?' His younger brother, Sakis, slid a glance at him.

Ari kept his gaze fixed ahead, jaw clenched tight. 'It's her husband's funeral. I'd have thought it was obvious she's *drowning in grief.*' How bitter those words tasted in his mouth. Because he knew they were the last emotion Perla Lowell was feeling. A woman who could do what she'd done with him forty-eight hours before putting her dead husband in the ground?

No, grief didn't even get a look-in.

Whereas he... *Theos.*

His gut clenched hard at the merciless lash of memories. He'd gorged himself on her, greedy in his need to forget, to blank the pain that had eviscerated him with each heartbeat.

Turning away from the spectacle playing out on the altar, he followed the trickle of guests who'd started to leave the chapel.

'Are you sure that's all?' Sakis demanded. 'I could've sworn she totally freaked out only when she saw you.'

Ari rounded on him as they exited into dappled sunshine. 'What the hell are you talking about?'

'I don't know, brother, but she seemed to be fixated on you. I thought maybe you knew her.'

'I've never been to this backwater until today, and I only came because *you* insisted you couldn't make it. What are you doing here, anyway?'

'It was my fault. I insisted.' Brianna, his beautiful soon-to-be sister-in-law spoke up. 'I thought, as Lowell's former employer, Sakis should be here. We tried to call you to let you know but your phone was off and the staff at Macdonald Hall said you'd checked out yesterday.'

His jaw clenched harder at the reminder.

He'd been running a fool's errand, desperately trying to track down the woman who'd run out on him in the middle of the night. A day and a half, he'd driven up and down the damned countryside, searching for the Mini whose red paint was a poor match for the vibrant hair colour of the woman who'd made him lose his mind and forget his pain for a few blissful hours.

Theos! How could he not have seen that it was all an illusion? They said sex made fools of men. They'd said nothing about the deadly blade of memory and the consequences of a desperate search for oblivion.

Bringing his mind into focus, he lowered his gaze away from his brother's blatant curiosity.

'We've paid our respects, now can we get the hell out of here?' he rasped.

Sakis nodded at a few guests before he answered him. 'Why, what's the hurry?'

'I have a seven o'clock meeting first thing in the morning, then I fly out to Miami.'

Sakis frowned. 'It's only two o'clock in the afternoon, Ari.'

His body didn't know that because he'd been up all day and all night, searching…chasing a dream that didn't exist.

He was losing it. He needed to get out of there before he marched back into that tiny chapel and roared his fury at that red-headed witch inside.

'I *know* what time it is. If you want to stay, feel free. I'll send the chopper back to Macdonald Hall for you two.' He couldn't get out of here fast enough, although every single bone in his body wanted to confront the duplicitous widow and give her a hefty piece of his mind.

With a nod at his brother and Brianna, he cut his way through the gawping crowd, uncaring that his face was set in a formidable scowl.

From the corner of his eye, he saw a flash of red hair heading his way. Although anger rose up within him, it took a monumental effort not to turn his head and see if it was Perla.

Clenching his fist, he stalked faster towards his limo, the need to be gone a fierce, urgent demand.

'Arion, wait!' Her husky voice was almost lost in the cacophony of the funeral spectacle. And it *was* a spectacle. Morgan Lowell's starring role in his own death via a drug overdose had ensured the media would make a meal of his funeral, even with the scant facts they knew.

Ari froze with one hand on the car door. Slowly, he sucked in a deep breath and turned to face her.

The widow in black. How very apt.

The widow whose bright, fiery red hair shone in the daylight with an unholy, tempting light, the same way it had gleamed temptingly across his pillow three nights ago.

Against his will, his body stirred. Blood pounded through his veins, momentarily deafening him with the roar of arousal. Before he could stop himself, his gaze raked over her.

Although her dress was funeral black, demure, almost plain to the point of drab, he wasn't fooled. He knew what lay beneath, the hot curves and the treacherous thighs, the delight he would uncover should he…

No. Never in a thousand years would he bring himself to touch her. They'd come together in a moment he'd thought was sacred, monumentally divine. Instead, it'd turned out to be a tawdry roll in the hay for her.

'Hello…Arion. I'm guessing your surname is Pantelides.' Green eyes searched his with wariness.

'And I now know your full name is *Perla* Lowell. So tell me, what role are you playing here now? Because we both know the grieving widow routine is just a front, don't we? Perhaps you're silently amused because you have saucy underwear underneath that staid black?'

She gasped, an expression that looked shockingly like deep hurt flashing across her face.

Theos, how utterly convincing she was. But not convincing enough to make him forget he'd nearly lost his mind hanging on for dear life as she rode him with merciless enthusiasm a little over forty-eight hours ago.

'How dare you?' She finally found her voice, even though it shook with her words.

'Very easily. I was the guy you were screwing when you should've been home mourning your husband. Now what the hell do you want?'

Her complexion had paled but then her skin was translucent thanks to her colouring. And yes, his words had been cruel, deliberately so. But she'd sullied his own memory of what the date had meant to him for ever.

And *that* he found hard to forgive.

'I was going to apologise for the…um…small deception. And to thank you for your discretion. But I see I needn't have bothered. You're nothing but a vile, bitter man, one who sees nothing wrong in bringing further pain and anguish on an already difficult day. So if you were truly on your way out of here, I guess the only thing I have to say is *good riddance*.'

Ari hardened his heart against the words. She

was in the wrong here, not him. She was clearly deluded if she thought he had something to be ashamed of. Turning, he yanked the back door open.

Before he slid in, he glanced at her one last time. 'Have fun revelling in your role of grieving widow. But when the crowd is gone and you think of reprising your *other* role, be sure to stay away from Macdonald Hall. Before the hour's out, I intend to supply the management with your name and ensure you're never allowed to set foot in there again.'

Fugue state.

Perla was sure that perfectly described her condition as she drifted through the wake, shaking hands, accepting condolences and agreeing that yes, Morgan had been a lovely man and a generous husband. On occasion, she even smiled at a distant uncle or great-aunt's fond anecdote.

The part of her that had reeled at Ari Pantelides's scathing condemnation an hour ago had long been suppressed under a blanket of fierce denial with Do Not Disturb signs hammered all over it.

At the time, she'd barely been able to contain the belief that he thought her some kind of scarlet woman or a trollop who frequented bars in the hope of landing a hot body for the night.

She audibly choked at the thought.

Mrs Clinton, who'd faithfully stuck by her side once they'd returned to the house she'd shared with Morgan and now shared with his parents, gave her a firm rub on the back. 'You're almost there, dear girl. Give it another half hour and I'll start dropping heavy hints that you should be left alone. Enough is enough.'

She glanced at the old dear's face. Perla had never confided the true state of her marriage with Mrs Clinton, or anyone for that matter. The very thought of it made humiliation rise like a tide inside her.

But she'd long suspected that the older woman somehow knew. Seeing the sympathy in her old rheumy eyes, Perla felt tears well up in hers.

Suddenly, as if the bough had broken, she couldn't stop the tide of hot, gulping tears that rose from deep inside.

'Oh, my dear.' Warm arms hugged her, providing the solace she'd been so cruelly denied throughout her marriage. The solace she'd imagined she'd found in a luxury penthouse suite three days ago, but had turned out to be another cruel illusion.

'I'm sorry, I shouldn't…I didn't mean to…'

'Nonsense! You have every right to do whatever you want on a day like this. Propriety be damned.'

Hysterical laughter bubbled up from her throat but she quickly smothered it. When a glass containing a caramel-coloured liquid that smelled suspiciously like brandy appeared in front of her, she glanced up.

The exquisitely beautiful woman who'd introduced herself as Brianna Moneypenny, soon-to-be Brianna Pantelides, held out the drink, sympathy shining from her expertly made-up eyes.

Perla wiped her own eyes, acutely conscious that she was messing up the make-up she'd carefully applied to hide the shadows under her eyes.

'Thank you.'

'No need to thank me. I've helped myself to a shot too. This is the third funeral Sakis and I have attended in the last month. My emotions are beyond shredded.' She sat down next to Perla, gracefully crossed her legs and offered a kind smile. 'It's nothing compared to what you must be feeling, of course, and if there's anything we can do, please don't hesitate to ask.'

'I…thank you. And please extend my thanks to your fiancé and…and the other Mr Pantelides for taking the time to come…' Perla's voice drifted off, simply because she couldn't think straight when her mind churned with thoughts of Arion Pantelides and the accusations he'd thrown at her. And even though she'd seen him get into his car, she couldn't stop her gaze from scouring the room, almost afraid to find out if he'd returned to tear a few more strips off her.

'Arion has left but I'll let him know,' Brianna said. A quick glance at her showed a sharp intellect that made Perla hope against hope that the other woman wasn't putting two with two and coming up with the perfect answer.

As it was, Perla felt as if she had the dreaded letter *A* branded on her forehead.

'Of course. I appreciate that he must be busy.' She didn't add that, in the light of what Morgan had done, they were the last people she'd expected to attend his funeral. Instead, she took a hasty sip of the brandy for much needed fortitude, and nearly choked when liquid fire burned down her throat.

'Well, he is. But he volunteered to come down here when he thought Sakis couldn't make it. And yet he seemed to have a bee in his bonnet about something. To be honest, it's the first time I've seen him that ruffled.' The speculation in her voice made Perla wish she'd worn her hair down to hide the colour rising in her face. 'It was quite a sight to behold.'

'Um, well…whatever it is, I hope he resolves it soon.'

'Hmm, so do I—'

'Brianna.' Sakis Pantelides chose that moment to approach them and offer his own condolences. Perla fought to find the appropriate response despite the nerves tearing through her stomach.

Then she watched as he turned to his fiancée, his face transforming with a very visible devotion that made Perla's heart lurch with jealousy and pain.

She'd long ago harboured hopes that someone would look at her like that. She'd foolishly believed that someone would be Morgan. Instead, he'd married her and blackmailed her into deceit and humiliation.

As an orphan, tossed from foster home to foster home all her childhood, she'd learned to mask the raw pain and despair of being the odd child that nobody wanted. But the hollow feeling in her belly had never gone away.

Meeting Morgan and suddenly finding herself the sole focus of his charm and wit had tricked her naïve self into believing she'd finally found someone who loved and cared for her, not out of duty, or because the state was paying them to do so, but because she was worth loving.

He'd roughly pulled the wool from her eyes within days of their wedding. But, even then, she'd foolishly believed she could salvage something from the only steady relationship she'd ever known. But weeks had dragged into months and months into years and by the time she'd accepted that she'd once again been cast aside, like a broken toy no one wanted to play with, it'd been too late to leave.

Her shaky breath drew glances from Sakis and Brianna but she couldn't look them in the face. She'd revealed so much already. She feared opening her mouth would be catastrophic, especially as she could feel Sakis Pantelides's keen gaze boring into her.

God, please don't let him guess what I did with his brother.

'I think it's time we left Mrs Lowell in peace, Sakis,' Brianna murmured.

Sakis nodded. 'My lawyers will be in touch with the paperwork regarding your husband's employment entitlements. But if you need anything in the meantime, please do not hesitate to get in touch.'

She glanced at him and immediately glanced away when his gaze narrowed.

He can't know!

Panic clawed at her. Surely Arion hadn't told him?

From the corner of her eye she saw Morgan's parents heading towards them. Clearing her throat, she fought the panic and pasted a suitable smile on her face.

No matter what had gone on between Morgan and her, Terry and Sarah Lowell had welcomed her into their hearts. She couldn't repay them with betrayal.

'I appreciate it, Mr Pantelides. Have a safe journey back to London.'

She turned away, grateful for the distraction that Morgan's wheelchair-bound mother brought to stop her wondering just what Sakis Pantelides knew about her carnal activities with his brother.

And she certainly couldn't think about Arion Pantelides and the heat that rushed under her skin every time she relived what had happened in his hotel room three days ago.

What had happened between them was now firmly in the past. Never to be repeated. What she needed to concentrate on now was picking up the shattered pieces and commencing the uphill battle that was the rest of her life.

CHAPTER FOUR

Three months later.

PERLA LOOKED UP for the umpteenth time as the Pantelides Inc. reception phone rang. The superbly groomed receptionist answered in dulcet tones and sliced another cool look at Perla before turning away.

Her teeth gritted and for a second she fought the urge to march over to the desk and demand she call upstairs again and get her the meeting she'd come here for.

Instead, she smoothed her hand down the black pencil skirt she'd spent her dwindling funds on and forced herself to remain seated. She'd turned up with no prior appointment, but only because her phone calls and emails had gone unanswered. And, truth be told, she'd only been waiting an hour and a half.

But being in the architecturally imposing building that bore the Pantelides name made her nerves jangle with each heartbeat, despite chastising herself that the likelihood that Arion Pantelides was in residence was negligible.

As the head of Pantelides Luxe, the branch of the conglomerate that ran its luxury hotels and casinos around the world—yes, she'd researched him in a moment of madness—Arion Pantelides spent very little time in England. And even if he were here, she'd asked for an appointment with the head of HR in Sakis's absence, not his brother.

So, really, there was no need for her to feel as if she were playing dare in an electric lightning storm.

Nevertheless, when the phone rang again, she held her breath. Expertly waxed eyebrows arched her way and a manicured hand motioned her forward.

Sighing her relief, Perla approached the desk as the receptionist hung up.

With another glance, which was now tinged with heavy speculation, the receptionist slid a visitor's badge along with a short silver key across the sleek glass counter.

'Please wear this at all times. Take the last lift on the right. Turn the key and press the button.'

Perla wanted to ask which floor she needed but she didn't want to look a fool, so she nodded her thanks and walked on shaky feet to the lift.

As it turned out, there was only one button to press. After inserting the key, she stabbed the green button that simply read *AP* and held her breath as the doors slid smoothly shut.

Her trepidation rose along with her meagre breakfast as she was whisked up at warp speed.

She barely had time to swallow the sudden nausea that assailed her before the lift doors were sliding open again. She started to step out, then froze as ice washed over her.

Arion Pantelides stood before her, tall, breathtaking, imposing…and as granite-faced as he'd been on the day she'd buried Morgan.

Perla swallowed. And swallowed again before she could speak. 'I think there's been some sort of misunderstanding. I'm not here to see you. I came to see your brother, my late husband's employer. Or, in his absence, I asked for the head of HR.'

'Sakis isn't here.' He confirmed what she already knew. 'He's on an extended honeymoon.' That voice, deep, husky, tinged with a haunting quality that she'd found intriguing since their first meeting, feathered along her nerves, sending her insides quaking with emotion so strong she wanted to take a step back from it.

Perla bit her lip. 'Yes, I know he got married last month but I didn't know he was still away… I was hoping he was back…' She drifted to a stop, her gaze trying desperately not to stray over his hauntingly beautiful face. A face that had featured in her dreams more times than she cared to acknowledge even to herself.

'He would've got married sooner. He delayed it because your husband's involvement in the Pantelides oil tanker crash was still under investigation. It would've been in bad taste to celebrate what is supposed to be the happiest day of any man's life with events like that hanging over everyone's head.'

The veiled mockery in his tone made her hackles rise, but it was the memory of his blistering anger the last time they'd met that made her insides quake.

She sucked in a deep breath. 'I apologise for the inconvenience—'

A slashing gesture with his hand stopped her words. 'He'll be back in two weeks. Feel free to come back then.'

The lift doors started to shut. Galvanised into action, she threw out a hand to stop it just as he did the same. Warm fingers grazed hers, sending electricity zapping through her. Perla jumped back and felt her heart thunder as she caught the look he levelled at her.

'I'm…I'm afraid this can't wait. Just point me in the direction of HR and I'll be out of your hair…'

As if reminded of that part of her, he stepped back and his lazy gaze trailed upward to rest on the hair she'd pulled back into a tight bun. Once he'd looked his fill, those hazel eyes, whose mesmerising flecks she recalled so vividly, recaptured hers. 'The whole HR team is on a day's training in Paris.'

Her stomach plummeted with despair. 'You're kidding, right? The *whole* team?'

He raised a brow at her.

'This really is an emergency. I came here specially. I need to talk to someone.'

Just like that, he shrugged, turned and walked away.

With every fibre of her being she wanted to let the doors shut once more and be plunged back to the ground floor, back to safety. But too much depended on her trip here today. Much too much.

So she took one step into Arion Pantelides's vast, opulent domain.

The architecture of the Pantelides Tower had looked formidable and stunning from the outside. Inside his office, the glass, chrome and steel structure blended with earthy tones made the place simply magnificent.

A wide roll-top desk, obviously an expensive antique, took up one corner of the glass-walled room, offering a breathtaking view of the river and the iconic buildings across the water. Under her feet, a deep gold carpet muffled her tentative footsteps.

She managed to take that all in in the handful of seconds before Arion folded his leanly muscled frame behind his desk.

Fighting her rising irritation, she glanced back

at him. 'Did you hear what I said? I need to talk to someone. It's important.'

'By all means, if this can't wait, tell me what the problem is and I'll see if I can accommodate you.'

He was toying with her, like a jungle animal toying with her prey. But she would not give him the satisfaction of thinking he could pounce and annihilate her again without consequences.

Even though the need to turn tail and flee stalked through her, she held her ground. Because what other choice did she have? She couldn't exactly flounce out of here. Her situation was too dire. They needed a solution now or Morgan's parents would lose the house in which they'd brought up their son. After what they'd been through, Perla couldn't stand by and do nothing whilst they suffered another blow in addition to the one they'd already been dealt by losing their only child.

Pursing her lips, she reached into her bag and brought out the file she'd compiled. Stepping forward, she slapped it on the table in front of him.

'According to these letters, neither Morgan's parents nor I are entitled to his death-while-employed insurance pay out. That can't be right. I know he signed on for that benefit.'

Arion steepled his fingers and watched her dispassionately over them. 'Ah, so you're here to collect on your husband's death.'

She couldn't stop herself from flinching at his

tone. And he saw it because his eyes gleamed with something akin to satisfaction.

She straightened her spine. 'I'm only asking what is rightly due to me as the spouse of a man who died while employed by your brother's company. I've read the small print. I know my rights, so I'd thank you not to make me sound like a vulture, Mr Pantelides.' She kept her voice firm because she sensed that any weakness would be met with scalpel-sharp ruthlessness.

Abruptly, he sat forward. Even across his desk, his imposing figure dominated, enclosing her in his powerful aura and making her pulse race.

Steady breaths. Just breathe.

'Trust me, *glikia mou*. No red-blooded man would look at you and liken you to a vulture. There are other, more exotic creatures perfectly apt to describe you.'

Really? Perla nearly groaned in relief when she realised she hadn't asked the question out loud.

'I'd prefer not to be thought of in terms of creatures great or small. Are you able to help me with this or am I wasting my time here?' she snapped.

Arion shrugged and glanced at his watch. 'Unfortunately, I have a lunch meeting in fifteen minutes.' He reached across and grabbed the papers from the table. 'Are you staying in town?'

She frowned at the unexpected question. 'No, I'm returning to Bath this evening.'

'Then don't let me stop you. Someone will be in touch soon.'

Something in the way he said that made suspicion rise higher. 'And just how soon is *soon?*'

Another careless shrug. 'I can get my brother to email his head of HR and get them to look into it but he's somewhere in the South Pacific. In a state of wedded bliss, who knows how often he checks his emails.' A shadow crossed his face, a tiny hint of what she'd glimpsed that night in the Macdonald Hall car park. Despite the need for self-preservation, her heart twisted.

'Arion…' He immediately stiffened and she bit her lip. *Wrong move, Perla! Keep on point.* 'Mr Pantelides, I don't have the sort of time you're offering. Could you…would you be willing to look into this yourself for me? Please?' she added when he remained frozen.

His eyes hardened. 'Is this where you trot out the for *old time's sake?*'

A heated flush crawled up her neck. 'No, I wouldn't be so crass as to refer to an occasion we'd both prefer to forget…but of course you won't believe that about me so I don't even know why I'm bothering. Look, I'm not sure whether you know about my circumstances, but Morgan and I lived with his parents after we got married. We were always going to move out and get a place of our own but that never happened. Two years ago, his mother was in a bad accident. Terry, Morgan's father, had to give up his job to look after her. Times have been hard for them. Without Morgan's insurance payment, they could lose their house. I know I'm nothing but a piece of trash in your eyes but they don't deserve to lose their home so soon after losing their son.'

She sucked in a breath and risked a glance at him. His expression remained stone-cold. For several minutes he didn't speak. Then he reached into his desk and slid across a small black triangular piece of gleaming plastic.

There were no markings on it. It could've been one of those if-you-had-to-apply-for-it-you-couldn't-afford-it credit cards reserved for multi-billionaires she'd read about in a magazine once. Or it could've been a loyalty card for die-hard coffee addicts. Perla had no way of telling. She looked from the card to Arion's face.

'What's that for?' she asked suspiciously.

'That card lets you into that lift.' He nodded towards the small lift to one side of his office, across from the one she'd come up in. 'The lift will take you straight to my penthouse. You'll wait for me there—'

'No way.' Perla stopped what was coming before he could finish.

His nostrils flared. 'Excuse me?'

'I won't do…whatever it is you have in mind. I know you think I'm nothing but some common whore but you're wrong. What happened between us that night wasn't cheap and it wasn't tawdry. Not for me at least. And I despise you for thinking I'd stoop that low to get you to help me—'

'Shut the hell up for one second and listen.' His rough command dried her words.

Her fist clenched. 'How dare you speak to me like—?'

'You said you have nowhere to stay. I have a meeting in…exactly eight minutes which will last for five hours. Minimum. Unless you intend to wander the streets in the rain until I'm finished, my offer is the best you're going to get.'

Surprise stamped through her. 'Oh, you mean you want me to go up and just…wait for you?' she asked.

'Why, Mrs Lowell, you sound disappointed.'

Severely taken aback, it took her a minute to regroup. 'I assure you, I'm not.'

He held out the card. 'Good.'

With a hand she cursed for trembling, she took it and headed slowly for the lift, trepidation in her every step.

'Oh, and Perla?' he murmured mockingly.

She stopped and turned back to him. 'What?'

'Don't look so frightened. You're not going up to a den of iniquity. There's more to my apartment than a bed and a pole for you to perform on.'

Her hand tightened on the card. 'Wow, I'm shocked you even have those. The way you've been acting, I'd imagine a torture rack and thumb screws would be more accurate furnishings for the women you send up there.'

His eyes darkened and the hand lying on the table clenched into a fist. She'd scored a point in their battle of wills. Finally. But the victory felt hollow. With every word and every gesture, Arion tainted their one night together, letting bitterness fill the space where she'd known a few hours of joy. If only she could forget. But forgetting was impossible. Not when he sat there, so vital, so impossibly gorgeous.

So infuriatingly captivating.

'I've never invited a woman to my penthouse. Ever.'

'Oh, then I'll consider myself one lucky woman. Don't worry, I'll try not to skip with joy and ruin your priceless floors.' She quickened her steps towards the lift, eager to be out of his sight and escape that merciless tongue. The plastic key slid soundlessly into the designated slot and the lift whispered open. She turned and faced the office, not in the least bit surprised to find Arion's gaze fixed squarely on her.

She wriggled her fingers in a careless wave. 'See you in a few hours, charmer.'

He didn't take his eyes off her, nor did he respond to her mockery as the lift door shut. But the look in his eyes sent a shiver of unease through her.

And with every hour that passed, despite having been whisked up into what felt like the lap of luxury—Ari's personal chef had served her the most delicious three-course meal, after which she'd had a call from the concierge to find out whether she wanted a facial or pedicure while she waited—her tension escalated.

So much so that when she heard the lift whisper open she stopped breathing. She jerked up from the suede sofa and her feet hit the floor with a thud. The magazine she'd been reading—one of many supplied by the concierge—spilled onto the floor. She bent to pick it up and straightened to find him a foot away, those piercing hazel eyes pinned on her.

'You...uh, do you have news for me?' she blurted, more to stem the overwhelming force of his presence than a need for immediate answers.

But then she didn't see the need for pleasantries. They weren't friends. Hell, they weren't even lovers. They were two strangers who'd given in to a mad moment that had returned to haunt them with merciless cruelty.

'Is that how you greeted your husband when he returned from work?' he rasped.

Her shocked gasp made him freeze. She watched a contrite grimace cross his face.

'Forgive me, that was beyond tasteless,' he rasped.

'Not to mention extremely disrespectful. You

know nothing about my life with Morgan.' And she intended it to remain that way.

He clawed a hand through his hair. 'No, I didn't. I'm sorry.'

With jerky movements, he loosened then yanked his tie off and flung it on the sofa where she'd been sitting.

Not expecting his immediate apology, Perla was left floundering. 'Apology accepted,' she murmured, a little absently because suddenly she found herself wondering what it would be like to have a real husband come home to her.

A husband like…Arion?

Hell, no. They would drive each other homicidal within weeks.

But during that time too they would have hot, exquisite, mind-melting sex.

The heat that rushed over her made her take a step back and give herself a mental slap. She wasn't here to reminisce over dreams that wouldn't come true in a million years. She was here to save Terry and Sarah's home—*her home*—before the bank made good on their threat of repossession.

Focus.

But then how could she, when Arion, having discarded his tie, was now in the process of undoing his top buttons, revealing the gloriously sleek muscled chest she'd explored without shame or inhibition a little over three months ago?

He caught her stare and a look passed through

his eyes. One she didn't want to interpret. One that made her rush to speech.

'I'm sorry if I seem to be rushing you but I'm hoping to catch the last train back to Bath tonight.'

He sauntered over to the drinks cabinet and poured a large whisky. She shook her head when he indicated the extensive array of drinks with a lifted brow.

She needed to keep her wits about her. The memory of what had happened the last time she'd shared a drink with him was a reminder never to indulge around him. Ever.

'I had Sakis's people look into it.'

'And?'

He knocked back the drink without taking his eyes off her. 'You said he signed the part of his contract that allows you to receive spousal income on his death?'

'Yes.'

'So you're not aware he signed the Under-Forty waiver thereafter?' he asked.

Unease dredged through her stomach. 'What's an *Under-Forty waiver?*'

'All employees under forty can take the option of death insurance or a yearly double bonus in place of compensation to family on death. Once an employee turns forty the option is no longer available. Your husband was—'

'Morgan was a long way from forty when he died,' she supplied through numb lips.

Ari nodded. 'According to his line manager, he asked for that clause to be amended in favour of receiving the double bonus and he never reinstated the original clause. Therefore, you are not entitled to receive funds.'

Ari watched her expression go from shock to disbelief to anger, then back to disbelief. She opened then shut her mouth. Then her gaze narrowed suspiciously.

'Please tell me you're not toying with me or making this up because…because of…'

'For someone who seems intent on making me believe our incident is behind you, you seem to leap back to it at the slightest opportunity.'

'I wasn't… I just…I can't believe Morgan would do that to his parents.'

To his parents. Not to her. The curious statement set off alarm bells in his brain. He didn't like alarm bells. They reminded him that he'd refused to listen to them clanging long and hard in the years before his father's real character had been brought to light.

They reminded him that in the end he'd lived in false hope that the father he'd looked up to wouldn't attempt to throw him to the wolves to save himself.

'You think that the husband you were so happy to betray was less than honest with you? Need I point out the irony there?' he bit out more sharply than he wanted to, the memory of betrayal and devastation growing rawer by the minute.

'I didn't betray Morgan.' Again an expression a lot like pain crossed her face. He hardened himself against it. Much like he'd hardened himself against thinking about her all the way through his meeting. A meeting he had barely been able to control because he hadn't been able to tear his mind away from the fact that she was here, in his living space, touching his things, leaving the hypnotically seductive scent of her body all over the place.

Theos, what had he been thinking, offering her the use of his apartment when he could just as easily have sent her across the street to the luxury guest apartments they used for visiting executives? Because he hadn't wanted to risk her strutting into another bar, catching the eye of another hungry predatory male and offering them a taste of what she'd offered him.

Stasi!

The admonition did nothing to lift his mood. 'I have no interest in lying to you, nor do I take pleasure in prolonging this meeting. You came here seeking information. I've provided it. What you do with that information is now up to you. I suggest you come clean with your in-laws and find a way around it.'

Her eyes darkened further as she stared at him.

'*Find a way around it*, just like that? You think it's that easy?'

He shrugged. 'I fail to see how any of this is my problem.'

She raised both hands and slid them through her long vibrant hair—hair she'd released from its tight bun at some point in the last few hours.

Ari found himself helplessly following the seductive ripple. Heat speared through him as he watched her pace to the window and back to where he stood, her agitated, breast-heaving breathing doing incredibly groin-hardening things to him.

She glared at him, the beginning of fire sparking those amazing green eyes. 'Surely I should've been informed of this change in his contract since I stood to lose from the amendment?' she railed at him.

The blatant statement of avarice made bitterness surge through him. Arion's father had torn their family apart, ripped it from its very foundations. All because of greed for money, carnal pleasure and power.

In the three months since his last encounter with Perla, he'd tried to blot the chaotic memories her actions had brought from his mind. He'd told himself that reacting to her the way he had at Macdonald Hall was because he'd been caught on the raw.

But, watching her now, he felt the same insidious desire creeping through him, damning him for being weak and helpless against his body's reaction to her.

When he'd finally been brought to justice, his father, although he hadn't shown an ounce of contrition, had confessed that he hadn't been able to help himself in the face of temptation.

A wave of despair washed over Ari now as he contemplated that perhaps he had a similar trait.

Hell, no!

But even that thought wasn't enough to stop his gaze from dropping to the hectic rise and fall of Perla's breasts as she paced his living room.

An image of her perfect rosy nipples and how they'd tasted in his mouth smashed through his mind.

Smothering the recollection, he took a few, much needed steps to his bar. 'It is what it is. Have you eaten?' he asked, then wondered why he was prolonging this meeting.

She dropped her hands, her expression incredulous. 'My life is in tatters and you're asking me if I want to eat?'

'Cut the melodrama. I was merely attempting to be courteous. I have nothing else to say to you on the matter of your husband's employment. Feel free to leave. Or stay and join me for dinner.' His hand tightened around the decanter as the invitation slipped out, almost without conscious thought.

'Why do you snarl every time you say the word

husband? Morgan was your brother's tanker pilot, and I know things didn't end well…'

Ari raised a brow. 'You think things didn't *end well?*'

He knew Sakis had done a stellar job in saving the company's reputation and hidden the true extent of Morgan Lowell's sabotage from the press. But was she also oblivious to her husband's betrayal? Or had she merely blinded herself to her husband's true nature, the way she'd blithely hidden the fact that she was newly widowed when she'd climbed into his bed?

'I'm not trying to belittle what happened. I just don't understand why you look as if you have dog poo on your shoes whenever I use the word *husband!*'

'Perhaps I don't wish to be reminded of the dead.' Death had brought too much suffering, had left devastation in its path, wounds that could never be healed. Knowing it was death that had made their paths cross in the first place didn't ease the vice around his chest.

His answer seemed to sober her. 'No, neither do I,' she said.

Her steps were decidedly less agitated when she went to retrieve her large bag from the corner of his sofa.

She was leaving, walking out of his life again. That single thought sent a spark of fierce rebellion through his stomach. He didn't realise he'd placed himself between the lift and her until she stopped in front of him.

'Thank you for your help, Mr Pantelides.' Her words were polite enough and her eyes were determined enough but he didn't miss the slight wobble to her mouth.

Ari wanted to slide his thumb over that mouth, loosen it until its velvet plumpness slid smoothly against his skin.

'What are you going to do?' he asked.

Her eyes narrowed. 'I thought you didn't care?'

'People tend to get litigious in your circumstances. For your own sake and the in-laws you claim to care about, I would hate for you to take that route.'

She hitched her handbag up onto her shoulder, her eyes back to full glare. 'I detect a veiled threat in there. But, from where I'm standing, I have nothing to lose so I may or may not speak with a lawyer to weigh my options.'

'From where I'm standing, you have none. Do you have a job?'

Her gaze slid away and he got the distinct feeling she was about to be less than truthful. 'Kind of.'

'Kind of? Doing what?'

She carefully avoided his gaze. 'Oh, this and that. Not that it's any of your business.'

'And does *this and that* not provide you with enough to keep a roof over your head?'

Her eyes darted back to his, defiance burning in their depth. 'If you must know, I'm not working at the moment. But I had a job before I got married. Morgan encouraged me to take a leave of absence for a while so his mother wasn't left alone for long periods of time. Terry was a long-haul lorry driver.'

'Right, so your husband convinced you to abandon your career to play babysitter to his mother. And you agreed?'

'There's that tone again. Why the hell am I even bothering?' She tried to move past him. 'Goodbye, Mr Pantelides. I hope you don't get a nosebleed from that super lofty position on your high horse.'

He caught her by the waist. The slide of her cotton shirt over her skin reminded him of how it'd felt to undress her, to bare her softness to his touch. Ari's mouth watered with the fierce need to experience that act again.

Weak... Theos, he was weak, just like his father.

'Let me go.'

'No,' he said, feeling a thread of real fear in that word. He should let her go. Forget about her. Forget how she'd made him feel that night. Because everything that had come after that moment of bliss had brought him nothing but jagged pain.

'Yes! I refuse to talk to you when you act like I'm some lowlife who's wandered into your perfect little world.'

'The circumstances of our meeting—'

'Can be placed squarely at your feet. I told you to leave me alone in that bar. But you were too busy playing the alpha *me-big-man-you-little-woman* role to listen to me. If you'd left me alone to have my drink we wouldn't be in this position.'

He whirled and propelled her back against the wall next to the lift. He didn't like that description of him. Didn't like that he'd seen what he wanted and just gone for it. It struck too close to home, made him too similar to the man he'd desperately tried to forget all these years.

And yet, as if from another dimension, he heard his reply. 'You mean this position when all I can think about is tearing that prissy little skirt off you, yanking aside your panties and slamming inside you?'

Her gasp was hot on his face. He welcomed it. Welcomed the excuse to plunge his tongue between her lips and taste her the way he'd been longing to taste her since she'd walked into his office today.

She pushed frantically at his shoulders but Ari wasn't in the mood to be denied. Not until he'd taken a little bit of the edge off this insane, pulsating need. Besides, her lips had started to cling, to kiss him back.

He groaned as her tongue dashed out to meet his, tentatively at first, then with progressively daring thrusts that made his blood rush south with dizzying speed. He hitched her higher up on the wall, felt her moan vibrate through them as he palmed her breast.

God, she was hot. So damned hot. Her nipples were already hard nubs beneath his thumbs as he teased them. Her cries of pleasure made him thankful she was here with him, not in a bar somewhere being hit on by other men.

Her fingers scraped over his nape and up through his hair, then dropped back down to restlessly explore his shoulders.

Theos, she was as hungry for him as he was for her.

With impatient fingers he slid up her skirt. The scrap of lace he encountered made his blood boil some more. With a rough growl, he shredded them.

'Oh, God! I can't believe you just did that,' she gasped and stared down at the tattered lace in his hand.

'Believe it. My hunger for you is bordering on the insane, *glikia mou*. Be warned.' He took her lips in another kiss, bit down on the plump lower lip and felt her jerk with the sensation.

Without giving her time to think, he sank to his knees and parted her thighs.

Her eyes widened as she read his intention. 'Arion...'

He hadn't had time to explore her like this last time. But this time he fully intended to gorge on her.

'No,' she said, but he could read the excitement in her eyes.

He managed to drag his lips from the velvet temptation of her inner thigh and the seductive scent inches away. 'Why?'

'Because you'll hate yourself if we do this again. And you'll hate me. For whatever trivial reason, you think I soiled something for you by sleeping with you three months ago. Frankly, I don't want to have to deal with whatever that was again.'

The reminder sent a spear of ice and jagged pain through his heart. Before he could stop himself, he rose and his hand slid to her throat.

Her eyes widened, not with fear, but with wariness at the look he knew was on his face. Every condemning thought he was trying to keep at bay came flooding back.

'*Trivial?* You think my reason for blaming you for sullying that day is *trivial?*' Pain made his voice hoarse, his heart thud dully in his veins. He distantly registered the quickening pulse beneath his palm but he was too lost in his own turmoil to react to it.

'I don't know! You never told me why. You were only interested in shredding me for—'

'For sleeping with a soulless wanton and ruining my wife's memory for ever?'

CHAPTER FIVE

PERLA FELT THE blood drain from her face. From head to toe she went numb. So numb she couldn't move. Or speak. Or do anything apart from stare at the pain-racked face of the man who held her upright.

When the full meaning of his words sank in, she jerked from him, pushing him back with a strength that felt superhuman but only made him take one single step back.

'Your *wife?* You…you're *married?*' The word choked out of her throat.

His nostrils flared and the skin around his mouth whitened. 'Was. Same as you. Bereaved. Same as you. The night we met, I was mourning. *Unlike* you.'

The accusation slashed across her skin, waking her numbness. The tingle of pain came with a healthy dose of anger. 'What makes you think I wasn't in mourning too?'

'Let me see, you were discussing cocktails with

the bartender and doing nothing to bat off his very clear interest in you.'

'And you think that automatically makes me less of a person? Because I wasn't snarling at a total stranger?'

'Your actions weren't those of a bereaved widow.'

'Everyone handles grief differently. Just because you chose to sit in a corner nursing your whisky and demanding silence doesn't mean you have the monopoly on heartache.'

She watched his face harden further. 'And what of the events afterwards? Which step of the grieving process did you tick by sharing the bed of a stranger before your husband was even in the ground?'

Despite her reeling senses, she fought to keep her voice steady. 'That's what bothers you, isn't it? The fact that I committed some cardinal sin by seeking solace before I'd buried my husband.'

'Was that what you were doing? Seeking solace?' His gaze bored into her, almost as if he was willing her to answer in the affirmative.

Because that would make him see her in a better light?

She shook her head and started to straighten her clothes. 'Does it matter what I say? You've already judged and found me guilty. I slept with you three days before my husband was in the ground. Trust me, you don't detest me more than I detest myself. But tell me, what's your excuse? Why did you sleep with me, other than that I was a willing body with a fascinating hair colour you couldn't resist?'

Her question made him jerk backward. He frowned and slowly his hand fell away from her throat. Hazel eyes dropped to his hand, and she watched it slowly curl into a fist, then release.

'For some of us, the pain reaches a point when it becomes unbearable. You were there. You offered a willing distraction.'

For some of us...a willing distraction...

Perla wasn't sure which of the two statements hurt deeper. What she was sure of was that Arion believed both statements; believed she'd gone to the bar at Macdonald Hall for her own selfish reasons other than with grief in mind.

And, in a way, wasn't he half right? The actions that had propelled her out of her car had had more to do with her frustration and anger at what Morgan had done to her than with pure grief.

The grief had come later, of course. Because, despite everything else he'd put her through, his loss hurt the two people she'd come to see as surrogate parents.

Terry and Sarah had partly filled a void she'd longed for Morgan to complete. They'd treated her as their own, and for someone who'd known only the coldness of the state foster system for most of her life, it'd been a blessed feeling to finally be part of a loving family. To feel a degree of being wanted she'd never experienced before.

Of course, she couldn't tell Arion that; he wouldn't believe her. She'd all but thrown herself at him in that car park, just after prattling on about Santorini and weddings.

She knew her actions had fallen far short of that expected of a newly bereaved wife. But she refused to let him keep denouncing her as a whore.

'I went into that bar for a drink, nothing else. I've never picked up a man in my life. You were a mistake that shouldn't have happened. But you happened. We had a moment. You can choose to shame me over it for as long as you live if it makes you feel better. I prefer to put it behind me, forget it ever happened.'

Hazel eyes narrowed and her breath caught. She'd been trying to reason with him. Instead, she'd made him angrier.

'If you wanted to forget you shouldn't have come here today. You should've appointed a representative and made them deal with this situation on your behalf. Coming here and parking yourself in my lobby tells me forgetting was the last thing on your mind.'

'You're wrong! Besides, I live in the real world, Mr Pantelides. Representatives and lawyers cost money. Hiring one to do the job I was perfectly capable of doing myself is irrational. The only thing this trip's cost me is a train ticket.'

One smooth eyebrow rose. Then his hand glided back to her neck, then down to her shoulder to rest just beneath her breast. 'Are you sure?' His breathing had grown slightly ragged and his other hand was now flexing through her hair, toying with it.

'Mr Pantelides—'

'You once told me my given name pleases you,' he murmured in that deadly low voice.

Her breath hitched. 'How can I forget if you keep reminding me?'

'Perhaps I don't want you to forget. Perhaps I want you to relive the pain and devastation and the pleasure with me.' One thumb teased her nipple and she felt her knees give way. 'If I have to be like *him*, then maybe I deserve whatever I get.'

The rawness in his voice struck deep inside her. 'Like who?'

He shook his head. 'No one. We've already committed the crime, Perla *mou*. The guilt will never leave us.'

Sensation bombarded and it was all she could do to keep her thoughts straight. 'So your solution is to commit the crime again?'

'If you'd stayed away, that would've ended the matter. But you're here now, front and centre, and I find that I lack the willpower to let you walk away.'

Her shocked laughter scraped her throat. 'You speak as if I have some sort of power over you—'

'You enthralled me from the moment I saw

you.' The words were spoken with no pleasure. None. There wasn't even a hint of a compliment in there.

'I'm sorry I affect you that way. Let go of me and I'll remove myself from your presence.'

His laugh was self-deprecatory. 'I've had you wedged against this door for the last twenty minutes. A gentleman would've offered you a drink, shown you the spectacular view from the tower deck, then offered to have you chauffeured home.'

'There's absolutely nothing stopping you from doing that.'

'But there is. Perla, I'm not a gentleman. Your panties are shredded at my feet and in the next sixty seconds I intend to be deep inside you.'

The words murmured, hot and urgent, against her neck made her close her eyes against the drugging inevitability that assailed her. Need, ten times more powerful than she'd experienced the first time with him, shot to her sex, leaving her drowning in liquid heat.

Perla barely managed a squeak when he swung her up in his arms and strode purposefully down a hallway. He stopped at the first door on his right and thrust it open to reveal a large white-carpeted bedroom. Black and chrome stood out in sharp contrast to each other, with no warmth or decorative aesthetics to lighten the mood.

He deposited her on the bed and pulled off her skirt, then froze. His mouth worked soundlessly for several seconds before the groan exploded from his chest.

'I thought I imagined how exquisite you were but I didn't.' Again the words were spoken with a starkness that caused a sliver of ice to pierce her pleasure.

'Arion…'

He rubbed the back of his knuckles across her sex, then stepped back and undressed with swift, jerky movements.

Pulling her thighs wide apart, he muttered something in his native language, his fingers biting into her thighs.

Sucking in a needy breath, she glanced up at him and almost wished she hadn't.

He looked tortured, his face a hard mask of desire as he surged inside her. He'd already damned himself by sleeping with her the first time.

They were caught in a spell neither seemed capable of breaking, and she watched that knowledge eat him alive as he penetrated deeper inside her.

'Ari…' It felt wrong, but it also felt so right, just like it had the first time.

The need to pull him back from his torment, if only for a moment, made her reach for him.

She touched his face and he refocused on her. Hazel eyes stared deep into hers as he increased the tempo of his thrusts. Almost possessed, he took her pleasure to another level. By the time her orgasm tore through her, she believed she'd touched something sacred. With a guttural cry, he followed her into ecstasy. Deep convulsions ripped through him as he collapsed on top of her. Her hand slid from his face to cradle his sweat-slicked neck. She shut her eyes as sensation drifted into calm. She knew it was elusive; that what they'd done was in no way calming or solace-giving.

They'd given in to their animal instincts. Had let that damning temptation run free. And yet…

Before she could complete the thought, he surged upright and swung himself off the bed. Keeping his back turned, he pulled on his boxers and trousers.

'The bathroom's through there. Get dressed and come and find me. We need to talk,' he threw over his shoulder before he left the room.

Dazed and confused, she lay there for several minutes, staring at the beautifully designed chrome ceiling lights. It took several deep breaths and a severe talking-to before she managed to pull herself together.

She returned to the living room to find him at the window, still shirtless and breathtakingly gorgeous.

He turned at her entrance and raked a hand through his hair. 'Are your in-laws expecting you back tonight?' he asked, his eyes exhibiting none of the tormented pleasure she'd witnessed minutes ago.

'Yes,' she responded warily, wondering where he was going with his enquiry.

He nodded. 'Then I'll make it fast. Pantelides Inc. has been through a lot in the past few years. I don't wish to draw any more unwanted attention to the company.' He went to the desk and picked up a pad and pen.

'Write your account details on here. I'll have funds transferred to your account first thing in the morning.'

The pain she'd been holding in a tight ball since she got up from his bed burst into her chest. 'Excuse me?' she rasped.

'I'm not unsympathetic to the fact that your husband left you in dire straits. I'm trying to make some form of reparation,' he replied, his voice still devoid of emotion.

'By sleeping with me and immediately offering me money afterwards?' Her own voice was sickeningly shaky and pain-filled but she didn't shy away from it. She wanted Arion Pantelides to know exactly what she thought of him. 'Why don't you come right out and book me for a repeat performance next Tuesday?'

His jaw tightened. 'What happened tonight won't happen again.'

'*Hallelujah!* Finally, something we both agree on. I thought you were pretty vile to accuse me of

the things you accused me of before. But this...
this is a new low.'

His grip tightened around the pad until it buckled beneath his strength. His gaze lowered but the rigid determination in his face didn't abate. 'Okay, perhaps the timing is unfortunate—'

'*You think?*' she snapped.

'But the offer remains. It's your choice whether to accept it or decline.'

'You can shove your offer where the sun doesn't shine!' She stalked past him to where she'd dropped her bag what felt like a thousand years ago. Snatching it up, she marched to the lift and pressed the button. Nothing happened. She stabbed harder, feeling her chin wobble with impending tears.

Dear God, no! No way was she going to cry in front of him.

'You need this.'

She turned. He was holding up the triangular card he'd given her earlier. She went to snatch it from him but he pulled it back at the last second.

'Perla—'

'No, don't say my name. You lost the right to speak to me when you offered me money for sleeping with you, you disgusting bastard.'

'Stop and think for a moment. The two situations have nothing to do with one another. You're being melodramatic again.'

'And you're being a complete ass who is holding me here against my will.'

'Think rationally. It's almost midnight. You're putting yourself in danger by attempting to return home at this time of night.'

'After everything you've said to me, you expect me to believe my safety concerns you?' She gave a very unladylike snort and glanced pointedly at the lift.

'Perla—'

'The only thing I want from you is to make the lift work, Ari. I want to leave. Right now.'

He sighed, and again she heard that weariness in his voice. 'I may not be a gentleman but I'm not averse to being schooled.'

She frowned when she realised he wasn't mocking her. He really meant it.

Turning, she faced him fully. 'First off, I wouldn't force a woman who wants to leave to stay against her will.'

He nodded, came forward and offered her the card. She took it.

'Second, don't ever, *ever* try to give a woman you've just slept with money. No matter your intention, it comes off as super sleazy.'

Hazel eyes gleamed before his eyelids veiled his expression. 'But your situation still needs to be addressed.'

'It's my problem. I'll take care of it.'

He took a deep breath and she couldn't stop her

eyes from devouring the sculpted chest that rose and fell. 'What were your skills before you gave up your career?'

The out-of-the-blue question threw her for a moment. Then she cleared her throat and tore her gaze away from the golden perfection of his skin. 'I was an events organiser for a global conglomerate.' She named her previous employer and his eyes widened a touch.

The fact that she'd managed to impress Arion Pantelides sent a fizz of pleasure through her.

'I'm leaving for LA in the morning but Pantelides Luxe has been on a recruitment drive for the last six weeks.' He scribbled a name and number on the mangled pad and passed it to her. 'If you're interested in interviewing for a job, call this number and speak to *my* head of HR.'

Unsure how to take the offer, she stared at him. 'Why are you doing this?' she finally blurted.

'I'm trying to find an alternative solution to your problem. Is this too not acceptable?' he asked, his face set in its usual world-weary lines.

'It's acceptable but I'm not sure it's the right solution for me.'

He shoved his hands into his trouser pockets. 'From where I'm standing, your options are slim to nil. Don't take too long in deciding or you'll find yourself back to square one.'

'Okay…thanks.' Her limbs felt heavy as she turned away. She told herself it was because she was drained from the head-on collision with Arion, and not the disconcerting realisation that she didn't want to leave. Because *that* would be ridiculous.

She slid the card through its slot and heard the smooth whirring of the lift.

'May I make another suggestion?' he asked. The sensation of his breath on her neck told her he'd moved close. Far closer than was good for her equilibrium.

She glanced over her shoulder. Up close, his sexy stubble made her want to run her hand over his jaw, feel its roughness just one more time. 'What?' She forced herself to speak.

'Allow my driver to get you back home?'

The thought of slogging through the rain to catch the last train to Bath made her waver dangerously. The sudden realisation that she could be doing so minus her panties made her stomach flip over.

She could stand on principle and endure a hugely uncomfortable journey, or she could give in this once. 'Okay.'

'I'll give him a half hour heads-up. It'll give us time to eat something on the tower deck before you leave.'

It took all of two minutes the next day to realise she had zero options. And really, had her head not been full of singeing memories of what she'd done with Ari the night before, she'd have come to that realisation a lot sooner.

But as much as she'd tried to push the shocking events that had stemmed from her complete lack of control from her mind, the more the vivid memories had tumbled forth.

She'd slept with Ari Pantelides for a second time, even after his blistering condemnation of her reasons for doing so the first time. Almost a day later, her internal muscles throbbed with the delicious friction of his possession.

But, even now, it was the vivid memory of his tortured face that haunted her.

Enough!

Perla glanced down at the piece of paper Ari had handed her. A quick call to a local lawyer this morning had reiterated Ari's warning. She had no recourse because Morgan had changed the terms of his contract.

Unless a miracle fell into her lap—and she was cynical enough to realise those were rarer than unicorn teeth—she and Morgan's parents were headed for the welfare office.

While her prior experience had been with only one large chain of hotels, she'd excelled at her job and enjoyed it enough to feel a tiny thrill at being given an opportunity to re-enter the business world again.

As for Ari…

According to her previous search, he was rarely

in London and therefore the chances that they would meet again were minuscule.

Ignoring the stab of discontentment that realisation brought, she grabbed the phone and dialled the number before she lost her nerve.

The swiftness with which her previous job history was taken and the interview scheduled left her floundering. As did the realisation that the interview itself would be spread over two days.

Feelings of insecurity started to rush back, a legacy, she knew, from her dealings with Morgan. Although she hated herself, she couldn't stop the feeling from growing.

When she found her fingers hovering over the phone an hour later, contemplating calling back to cancel the interview, she pursed her lips and straightened her spine.

Morgan might have succeeded in whittling away her self-confidence, through threats and blackmail, but giving in now would see her in the far more precarious position of being without means to support herself and his parents.

Besides, she was getting ahead of herself. Maybe she wouldn't even get this job—

No!

She might not believe in unicorns but neither would she succumb to doom and gloom. Taking a deep breath, she stepped back from the phone and went to find her in-laws.

Explaining to them why she had to return to

London again so soon was a little delicate, seeing as she'd told them the outcome of her previous visit. She didn't want to get their hopes up because she'd been out of the job market for far too long and knew realistically she could fall flat on her face the first time, positive thinking or not.

'Are you sure that's what you want to do? London is so far away,' Sarah said worriedly.

'Nonsense, it's only a short commute by train. And don't forget, we need all the help we can get right now. We wish you all the best, Perla. Don't we, Sarah?' Terry glanced at his wife.

Sarah smiled, her eyes brightening a little from the devastating sadness still lurking in their brown depths. 'Of course we do. It's just that…we don't know what we'd do without you now that Morgan is…' Tears filled her eyes and she dabbed at them with the hanky Terry slipped into her hand.

Perla felt her throat clog and quickly swallowed. *This* was the reason she'd stayed. The reason she'd kept Morgan's secret and given up her career.

Watching them console each other in their grief, the need to protect them surged higher. From the moment she'd been introduced to Terry and Sarah Lowell, they'd taken her into their hearts. After the devastation of Morgan's revelation, she'd known, just as he'd deviously surmised, that she couldn't turn her back on the only promise of a proper home she'd ever known.

Neither could she reveal the secret that would've destroyed his parents.

The familiar guilt for the secret she carried and could never share made her rise from her seat. 'I…I'd better go and brush up on my interview techniques.'

In the hallway, she paused for a second to steady her breathing. Then she straightened.

Morgan was gone. Terry and Sarah were her responsibility now.

Briskly, Perla entered her bedroom and busied herself sorting through her meagre clothes. Three interviews in two days meant she would have to be inventive with her wardrobe.

The black skirt and satin shirt she'd worn to London would have to make another appearance. As would the black dress she'd worn the night she'd met Ari.

Laying the garments on the bed, she couldn't help the treacherous bite of sensation that nipped at her. Both outfits held memories she'd rather forget, of Ari's hands on her body, undressing her, stripping her bare before taking her with masterful possession.

Heat flared high, making her fingers shake as she scraped back her hair and forced the memories away.

She had no business thinking about another man in this house; in this room. Even if that man was the only person in her life who'd made her feel special and wanted for a brief moment in time. Even if the memory of his face as he'd taken her forced feelings of protectiveness as well as desire to surge into her chest.

It was over and done with. Move on.

'Congratulations and welcome to the company.'

Perla heard the words from far off, still numbly disbelieving that she'd actually got through the gruelling interviews to secure a job on the Pantelides Luxe events management team.

'I...thank you.'

The two other candidates who'd also been offered similar jobs out of the twenty-five candidates wore similar expressions of pleased wonderment.

She'd got the job, with a salary and benefits that had left her mouth agape when she'd read them on her contract. Now she forced herself to focus as the head of HR continued to speak.

'For those who require the option, your first month's salary will be paid to you in advance of month's end. Just tick that option when you sign your contract. But remember if you should decide to leave the company before the first thirty days are up, you will be required to reimburse the company.' He looked directly at her as he said that.

Slowly anger and embarrassment replaced the stunned pleasure.

Had Ari Pantelides been so unprofessional as to share her private financial affairs with others?

It was bad enough that she'd seen the morbidly curious looks on a few of the employees' faces as she'd been introduced. She was well aware that the widow of the man whose actions had caused a Pantelides oil tanker to crash and pollute a breath-taking African coast only a few short months ago was the last person they expected to seek employment in this company.

Knowing that her financial dire straits were being shared with others made her skin crawl with shame.

Forcing her head high, she returned the older man's stare, barely hearing the end of his welcome speech as she tried to grapple with her emotions. Fifteen minutes later, contract in hand, she started to leave the room.

The low hum of her mobile had her rooting through her handbag.

'Hello?'

'I understand congratulations are in order.' The voice, deep and gravel-rough, sent a pulse of heat through her belly.

'I…how did you get my phone number?' she blurted to cover her inner floundering.

'You're now my employee, Perla. Prepare yourself for the fact that some of your life is now an open book to me.'

A shiver went through her at the low, dark promise. As much as she tried to tell herself she wasn't affected, his voice did things to her that were indecent. Her hand tightened on the phone. 'So open that you decided to share some of it with your HR director?' she demanded.

'Excuse me?'

'Did you tell your HR director that I needed money?' The very thought of it made her flush with mortification.

'Why would I do that?' He sounded amused. Vaguely it occurred to her that he didn't sound as tormented and as bleak as he had a few days ago. Why that thought lifted her heart, she refused to contemplate as she reminded herself why she was annoyed with him.

'Because he offered a month's salary in advance. I may have been out of the general workforce a while but even I know that salaries don't get paid in advance.'

'Did he offer only you that option?' he asked.

'No, he offered it to the other new employees as well.'

He remained silent for several heartbeats. 'The reason for that perk is because most of the people I hire for the role you're filling are young, dynamic graduates. *Broke*, young, dynamic graduates who I expect to hit the ground running. The last thing I want them to be thinking about is how to pay their rent or feed themselves. If and when I headhunt other talent, I offer them signing-on bonuses too. Either way, everyone gets the same treatment.'

The bruised hurt eased a little. 'Oh, so I wasn't singled out for special treatment?'

'Now you sound disappointed,' he mocked in a low tone that was equally as lethal to her senses.

'I'm not.' And of course, now he'd explained the reason for the stipulation, it made total sense. How better to keep his employees happy and loyal than to ease the one thing certain to add to their anxiety in their first months of employment? Realising there was something else she needed to do, she cleared her throat. 'Thank you…for giving me this opportunity. I promise I won't let you down.'

Again a thoughtful silence greeted her words. 'I'm glad to hear it, Perla, because I'm giving you the chance to prove it sooner rather than later.'

Her heart jumped into her throat. 'What do you mean?'

'It means I'm throwing you in at the deep end. You fly out to join me in Miami after your accelerated orientation tomorrow. My assistant will provide you with the details.'

CHAPTER SIX

TEN VIP GUESTS.

Miami Fashion Week.

What could go wrong? It turned out to be plenty as Perla doused yet another metaphorical fire four days later, this time in the form of a wardrobe malfunction for one of the guests—a social media mogul's wife, minutes before she was due to head down to the Pantelides V3 Hotel & Casino.

She curbed the urge to blurt out that she was an events organiser not a stylist and placed a phone call to summon the harried stylist. Twenty minutes later, after the crisis had been averted, the young blonde cast a grateful glance at Perla as they rode the lift down to the lobby.

'I should've gone for something like what you're wearing instead of this...this thing.' She indicated the blue organza multi-layered dress that showed off more cleavage and bare back than Perla would ever be comfortable showing.

Her own knee-length silk dress, although slashed dramatically at the waist and side, was covered with thin mesh netting that made her feel not quite so…exposed. And the long fitted sleeves made of the softest leather offered further boosting confidence.

'That black totally rocks against the vivid colour of your hair. You must give me the name of your colourist. Everyone tells me red and curly is the new black this season.' The blonde flicked her straight hair back and offered a brittle smile.

Again Perla bit her tongue, smiled back and discreetly checked her watch. The pre-runway show drinks would be served in exactly six minutes. Although she realised she was probably being rude by not responding and discussing her now extensive wardrobe that had come courtesy of her generous Pantelides clothes expense account, she couldn't think beyond the fact that in a few minutes she'd be coming face to face with Ari for the first time in almost a week.

By the time she'd arrived in Miami, he'd left for New York and she'd been given three days to prep for the arrival of the special guests, who ranged from a young senator to Hollywood royalty.

The earlier sailing trip around Biscayne Bay had been a success despite one guest almost ending up being launched overboard after one too many mojitos.

Keeping her fingers crossed for the same success tonight, she pasted a smile on her face as the lift doors opened onto the foyer that led to the cordoned-off VIP lounges where the runway shows were being held.

Ari Pantelides stood with a group of guests. Head and shoulders above most men, he was the first person she saw when she stepped forward.

The punch to her solar plexus winded her for an instant. Her mouth dried as she took in his imposing shoulders and breathtaking physique.

It really was a sin how one man could possess such a strikingly commanding presence. He turned to another guest and Perla caught a glimpse of that designer stubble. The memory of its roughness against her breasts and thighs sent a pulse of heat straight between her legs.

God, she really needed to get a grip. Like, right now!

Of course, he chose that moment to turn his head towards her.

Hooded eyes speared hers before they rose to rest on her hair. Recalling his fascination with her hair, she fought the foolish urge to touch the elaborate knot she'd worked the tresses into.

You're here to work!

The stern reminder focused her a little.

Turning to the blonde woman at her side, she said, 'I'll be around if you require anything else, Mrs Hamilton. Otherwise, I'll see you at the show in an hour.'

She left Selena Hamilton to find her husband and headed straight for the head waiter. After reassuring herself that everything was running smoothly, she found a quiet corner and activated her mini tablet. Double and triple-checking every detail was essential. The two designers whose shows they would be visiting were temperamental at the best of times and, with runway shows, seating arrangements could descend into chaos with little warning.

'*Kalispera,* Perla.'

Her hand trembled and she nearly lost her hold on her tablet as the deep voice washed over her. Her one visit to Santorini meant she understood the greeting.

Her head snapped up and her eyes collided with steady hazel eyes. 'Good evening, Ar…Mr Pantelides. How was your trip?'

His eyes narrowed slightly at the hasty correction but he didn't comment on it. 'Predictable. You seem to have settled in okay. I hear your boat trip today was interesting.'

It wasn't a question and she had very little doubt that he'd been checking up on her since her arrival.

'Yes, it hasn't been smooth sailing, pardon the pun, but the orientation was very useful. And your head of Events let me shadow him for a day to get the hang of things. That was useful too…' She stopped when she realised she was babbling. But, with him standing so close, she was dealt the full force of his powerful aura and the spicy scent of his aftershave. She'd smelled him up close and personal and knew continuing to breathe him in was not a very wise idea. 'Anyway, I need to get back to work.'

He stopped her with a brush of his fingers down her arm. Electricity shot through her body. 'How did your in-laws take your new status?' he asked.

She froze, looked at him to see if he was being sarcastic but his eyes only held mild interest. 'A lot better than some of the Pantelides employees.' She bit her lip at the slip. She'd meant to let the avidly curious looks and whispers behind her back slide right over her. But it'd been hard not to be affected.

Her stomach hollowed when his eyes narrowed. 'Who's been giving you a hard time?' he asked, his voice low and dangerous enough to send a shiver down her spine.

'Sorry, I didn't stop long enough to take names. Besides, can you really blame them? Morgan's actions nearly brought down your company.'

He stilled. 'So you know the full details of what he did?'

Perla frowned. 'Of course I know. Even though your brother tried to protect me from the whole truth, I got enough from the papers to put the pieces together. Frankly, I was surprised Morgan's benefits weren't stripped from him, all things considered.'

His jaw clenched for a moment before his face

cleared. 'Those benefits weren't advantageous to you in the end, though, were they? It must have been upsetting to find out that the man you loved would betray you that way?' This time there was a definite question in his tone. His incisive gaze bored right into her. As if he was trying to understand her. And, more specifically, her actions on the night they'd met.

To admit that she hadn't been thinking straight when she'd slept with him—least of all of her dead husband—would only make things worse. 'It's not easy to find out, no.' But compared to the bombshell she'd received on the night of her wedding it was a walk in the park.

'I'm aware that betrayal has a way of messing with people's minds.' A hint of that torment she'd glimpsed made an appearance. As did the curiously strong need to alleviate it for him.

Brushing it away, she answered, 'Are we talking people generally or do you have personal knowledge of this?'

He stepped closer, blocking out the rest of the room and giving her no choice but to inhale his scent, to look into those unique gold-flecked hazel eyes. 'I've been dealt a few life lessons but I'm talking about you. Was that why you slept with me?' he breathed with a quiet intensity. 'To assuage your sense of betrayal?'

'Why are we going over this again?'

He murmured something pithy under his breath.

'Perhaps I'm trying to make sense of it all. Trying to square things in my mind so I can move on.'

Shame scythed through her as she admitted that she didn't want it squared away. She wanted to remember that night; to treasure it as the special moment in time it'd been for her. Of course, she knew she could never tell him that.

Straightening her spine, she returned his stare. 'Morgan's decisions and actions were his own. For my part, I married him for better or worse; he was the man I'd pledged to honour and cherish. And yes, before you remind me again, I broke that vow before he was even buried. Was I upset that things turned out the way they did? Of course I am.' A trill of laughter from a guest grounded her to where she was. 'I also think that this is the last place we should be discussing this. Frankly, I'd prefer it if we buried the subject once and for all. Can we do that, please?'

He stared down at her for several minutes before he inhaled deeply. He took a single step back and nodded. 'Consider the matter buried.'

She managed to nod before glancing over his shoulder. Several guests were looking their way, no doubt wondering why she'd commandeered Ari's attention. 'I need to get back to work, earn the generous salary you're paying me.'

His lips pursed but he gave her enough room to slide past. 'I look forward to seeing you in action.'

Perla wasn't sure if it was a threat or anticipation. And she couldn't dwell on it because her insides were churning from the exchange. Once again, it had seemed as if her reason for sleeping with him mattered to him.

Far from being a distraction as he'd claimed, it seemed he couldn't stop thinking about that night any more than she could.

Could she trust him not to bring it up again? Could she trust herself not to blurt out that it'd meant more than just a means to alleviate her pain?

She sucked in a deep breath and pinned a smile on her face. She'd survived Morgan and the debacle that had been her marriage.

She was a lot stronger now for it. She just needed to keep reminding herself of it.

Both runway shows went without a hitch. Watching from the back, Perla breathed a sigh of relief when the lights went up and her guests started to finish off their vintage champagne. Another few minutes and she could start herding them back to the limos to return to the Pantelides Casino for the gambling part of the evening. That was the most important part because it was why Ari had organised this event in the first place—

'Relax,' Ari said from beside her. How could a man so big, move so silently? 'You're off to a good start if Selena Hamilton is singing your praises. According to her, the two of you are BFFs now.'

He picked up two glasses of pink champagne from a hovering waiter's tray and offered one to her.

'I wouldn't go that far but I'm glad she's pleased.' She took the champagne but didn't take a sip, much as she wanted to. The need for liquid courage was what had placed her in Ari Pantelides's crosshairs in the first place.

She was not going to make the mistake of drinking around him ever again.

'She isn't the only one who is impressed by your efficiency.'

Unable to help herself, she looked up at him. Hazel eyes captured hers and her breath snagged in her chest. 'Oh?'

'Her husband was equally effusive. Twice as much, in fact.' A hard bite had materialised in his tone.

She swallowed. 'What are you implying?'

He shrugged. 'He has wandering hands. Make sure you're not caught between them.'

On the surface, it seemed like a fair warning. Perhaps she was reading more into the situation than was necessary. They stared at each other for several heartbeats before she nodded. 'Thanks for the heads-up.'

His eyes flicked to her hair and again the punch of heat returned. Never in her wildest imagination would she have thought the colour of her hair would produce such a reaction. But every time Ari's gaze slid hungrily over her hair she felt hot, bothered and more than a little on edge. Before she could stop it, a small sound escaped her throat.

His gaze locked on hers once more. The air thickened around them, blocking the sounds of the party and locking them in their own sensual cocoon.

'Please, don't.' She was very much aware that she was begging. For as long as she could remember she'd wanted someone to notice her, give her a little bit of their time and attention. Although she'd found that to some extent with Terry and Sarah, it ultimately wasn't the right kind.

The attention Ari was giving her now *felt* like the right kind. Which was extremely frightening because it was the skull-and-crossbones kind, guaranteed to annihilate her with minimal effort.

'I'm as puzzled by my fascination as you are, *pethi mou*,' he murmured. 'Or perhaps my inner ten-year-old is still reeling from the discovery that his favourite TV actress's red hair came from a bottle,' he said dryly.

'How traumatic for you. Would it be better if I dyed my hair black or shaved it all off?' she half teased.

He sucked in a sharp breath and his grip tightened around his glass. 'I invite you to dare,' he breathed in a low, dangerous voice.

'You know, this would be the moment when I tell you that it's *my* hair, and I can do with it what I choose.'

'And I would in turn threaten to lock you up in a faraway dungeon until you came to your senses.'

Against her will, she felt a smile curve her lips. His mouth twitched too, as if sharing her amusement, but then his face turned serious again, and they went back to staring at each other.

Dirty, delicious thoughts of dungeons and shirtless heroes cascaded through her brain, sending spikes of desire darting through her body.

Realising just how pathetic she was being to take pleasure in the possessive tone in his voice, she cleared her throat. 'Can I make a suggestion?'

He took a sip of his drink without taking his eyes off her. She desperately wished she could follow suit but she needed to stay as clear-headed as possible. 'Go ahead.'

'Perhaps if we agree to stay out of each other's way, this...*thing* will eventually go away.'

'Haven't you heard the new saying? *Abstinence makes the heart grow fonder?*'

'I think we can both agree our hearts aren't the problem here.'

His face slowly froze until it was a hard, inscrutable mask. 'No. They're most definitely not.' The depth of feeling in his voice made something sharp catch in her chest. Again that torment stained his expression.

'You must miss her very much. Your wife,' she blurted before she could stop herself.

His fingers tightened so forcefully around the

stem of his glass she feared it would snap. 'Sofia's death is a loss to the world. And to me.' The agony in his voice cut right into her heart.

Unable to look into his face, bleak with pain and guilt, she glanced away. Her own fingers were curled around the warming glass of champagne which trembled wildly, threatening to spill its contents. Hurriedly, she set it down on a nearby table.

'I never got the chance to say it before. I'm sorry...for your loss. Um, please excuse me. I think I'm needed now.'

She hurried away before she could do or say something rash, like ask him to define what that kind of love felt like. Or expose the emotion writhing through her that felt shamefully like jealousy.

She'd wanted a love like that for herself, had built all her hopes around Morgan, who had taken her desperate need and used it to blackmail her. Fate had kicked her in the teeth for daring to hold out her hand and ask.

She wasn't foolish enough to even contemplate asking a second time. The lesson had been well and truly delivered.

Ari watched Perla walk away, stunned by what he'd just revealed. He never spoke about Sofia. Never. Not to his brothers, not to his mother. And certainly not to traitorous strangers he'd made the colossal mistake of sleeping with.

And yet, with one simple sentence, he'd spilled

his guts; would've spilled some more if Perla hadn't rushed away. Because the admission of how Sofia—a warm-hearted, gentle innocent whom he'd ruthlessly clung onto and used to soothe his ravaged soul right after his father's betrayal—had come into his life and ultimately left it, had been right there on his tongue.

Absently nodding to a guest who'd approached and started talking to him, he tried to reel in his flailing senses.

It was unconscionable that he still felt this unrelenting pull towards Perla Lowell. What had happened between them—twice—should've been enough to curb whatever appetites he hadn't even realised were growing until he'd met her.

At first he'd thought his fascination with her was because she was the first woman he'd slept with after Sofia. That had been his excuse in the weeks following his discovery of her real identity.

And the second time?

He gritted his teeth. The second time, their emotions had been running high. So high, he hadn't had the common sense to use a condom. Hell, even that little nugget hadn't hit him until he was halfway across the Atlantic on his way to the US. A shudder raced under his skin at the sheer stupidity of his actions.

How many times, growing up, had he cautioned his brothers on the responsibility of taking care of their sexual health and those of the women they slept with, especially after finding out the bitter and humiliating legacy their father had left behind?

Granted, both Sakis and Theo were old enough now and no longer his responsibility. But for him to have fallen in the same trap, under the same spell that—

Enough. Beating himself up about it would achieve nothing. He smothered his thoughts and concentrated on the guest next to him, expertly hiding his distaste when he saw who it was trying to get his attention.

'She's something, your new organiser.' Roger Hamilton's gaze was fixed on Perla as she spoke to his guests, her smile open and friendly. The clear interest in his eyes sent a bolt of anger through Ari.

'She's also off-limits.' The snarl in his tone was unmistakable.

Hamilton's eyes widened, then his thin lips curved in a sly, knowing grin. 'Right, she's marked territory. Got it, buddy.'

Ari gritted his teeth and opened his mouth to deny the assertion. 'Very marked. And I'm very territorial. Are we clear?' *Theos*, where had that come from? He was losing his mind. There was no doubt about that.

Roger slapped him on the arm. 'As crystal, buddy. But tell me something; between you and I, is that hair colour real?'

Ari's fists clenched so hard his knuckles screamed in protest. From the first, he'd found an almost unholy fascination with Perla's hair. To hear that same fascination in another man's voice made the blackest fury roll through him.

'That, *buddy*,' he breathed, 'is something you'll never find out.'

From then on, he made sure he kept a room's width between himself and Perla at all times. Not that he actively needed to. She seemed just as determined to stay away from him.

A thought that should've pleased him, but only succeeded in darkening his mood further. On impulse, he pulled his phone out of his pocket and dialled.

Theo answered on the first ring. 'A call from the big man himself. I haven't been naughty, have I?'

'You tell me. And while you're at it, tell me what the hell is so captivating about Rio that you can't seem to tear yourself from the place?'

His youngest brother laughed. 'Sun, sea and wall-to-wall gorgeous women. Need I say more?' Despite his tone, there was something cagey that set Ari's radar buzzing.

'Is everything okay, man?' The worry that never abated when it came to his brothers rose higher. Of all his family members, Theo had been the youngest and most vulnerable when their world had unravelled, thanks to his father. That worry had never gone away.

'Of course. How about you? Normally, you send me terse one-line emails asking me to report in.'

'Half of which you never answer. Thought I'd try another means to get your attention.'

Theo remained silent for a minute. 'You sure you're okay, bro?'

A flash of red caught his eye and he tensed further. 'I'm fine. But it would be good to row again, all three of us, some time soon.'

'Ah, you're nostalgic to get your ass whopped. I can oblige. But would this need to burn energy have anything to do with the headache you've created for yourself by hiring the Lowell woman?'

He gave an inward sigh. 'You've heard?'

Theo snorted. 'The whole company's wondering if you've lost your mind. Hell, *I'm* wondering if you've lost your mind. *Theos,* she's not blackmailing you in any way, is she?' he asked sharply.

The tense note in Theo's voice made Ari's hand clench over his phone as a wave of pain swept over him. Theo had been kidnapped as a teenager and their family held to ransom for a tense two weeks before he'd been released, which made the subject of blackmail a very volatile one.

'No, she needed a job, she proved to have the skill and I gave her one.'

'Did you run it past Sakis, because I'm pretty

sure he'll blow a gasket once he crawls out of his love cocoon and returns to the real world.'

Ari's jaw tightened. 'I'll deal with Sakis. In the meantime, have your assistant check schedules with mine about our next rowing session. I want to get together sooner rather than later, and get to the bottom of exactly what you're doing in Rio.'

'Dammit, anyone would think I was still twelve instead of a grown man.'

'You'll always be a twelve-year-old to me, brother, simply because you can't help but act like one.' He noticed the gruffness in his voice but couldn't help it.

He hung up to Theo's pithy curse and realised he was smiling. Pocketing his phone, he looked up and found Perla's gaze on him. Wide green eyes held shock and wonder, which she quickly tried to bank. When he realised it was in reaction to his smile, he cursed under his breath.

Was it really so strange that he would smile? Was he such an ogre that he'd given the impression that smiling was beyond him?

Yes...

A lance of pain speared his heart. Smiling and laughter had become a thing of the past for him, ever since he'd lost the most precious thing in his life through hubris and carelessness. He'd believed he'd paid enough, sacrificed enough for his family and deserved happiness of his own. He'd believed he'd bled enough to owe fate nothing else.

He'd been careless with Sofia's health, given in to her penchant to always look on the bright side, when deep down he'd known the bright side rarely existed. Guilt rose to mingle with the pain, wiping away every last trace of mirth from his soul. He had no right to smile or laugh. Not when he had blood on his hands…

Realising Perla was still staring at him, he turned away abruptly. But the unsettled feeling wouldn't go away.

Perhaps Theo had been right. Had he lost his marbles by employing her, despite her obvious talent? He knew had he looked harder, he'd have found someone equally talented to employ who didn't rock the boat or make his male clients salivate just by the sight of her. He pursed his lips. Hell, she herself knew she was distracting enough to have made some of his employees talk, made her own life uncomfortable—

Frowning, he removed his phone from his pocket and dialled his assistant. 'Contact my head of HR—I want a conference call first thing tomorrow. Tell him I want to discuss Perla Lowell.'

CHAPTER SEVEN

'WHY DID YOUR HR director just call to check up on me? And please don't tell me he does that with everyone else because I asked David and Cynthia and he didn't call them so I know I'm the only one he's called.'

Ari continued to admire the stunning penthouse view from his latest hotel set in the heart of Washington DC and forced himself not to react to the huskily voiced accusation or the unwanted intrusion. But it was difficult not to turn around; not to tense against the electricity that zapped through him at her presence.

It'd been three weeks since Miami, and the last time he'd seen Perla. He'd left the day after Fashion Week and busied himself with his other casinos and hotels on the West Coast. But he'd needed to return because Pantelides WDC was by far his most successful hotel yet and he needed to throw his every last waking moment into making it the jewel in the Pantelides Luxe crown.

That he'd spent far too much time thinking

about Perla Lowell was something he preferred to view as simply making sure she wasn't causing any more ruffles in his company. Of course, he'd have preferred if word hadn't got out that he was doing so but...

He sighed. 'Discretion really seems to be thin on the ground these days.'

Her gasp sounded just behind his left shoulder. He tensed further, bracing himself for the impact of the sight and scent of her.

'So you're not denying it? You do realise how you've made me look by doing that, don't you?'

'What exactly did my director say to you?' he asked.

'He asked me how I was getting on with work and with my colleagues.'

'And you immediately jumped to the conclusion that I was trying to undermine you somehow?'

'Did you or did you not ask him to call to check up on me?'

'Perla, you brought a potential workplace problem to my attention. And I took steps to rectify it. I think my director may have taken his directive a little too seriously given who you are. If you think it was an unnecessary step—'

'I do,' she flung at his back.

Ari gritted his teeth and tried to remain calm as she continued.

'Now you've said something—'

'Actually, *you* said something. Had you come

to me instead of seeking verification from your colleagues, they would've been none the wiser.'

'So you're saying this is my fault?' Outrage filled her voice. 'And can you turn around when I'm talking to you, please?' she snapped.

With another sigh, he started to turn. 'I think you're blowing things out of proportion—' He stopped dead when he caught his first glimpse of her.

Her hair was a long, dark, *wet* ribbon curling over her naked shoulder. And she wore a black bikini with the thinnest strings that looked as if they were about to succumb to the laws of gravity. Heat punched into his gut so viciously, he had to lock his knees to keep from stumbling backward against the floor-to-ceiling window behind him. Around her waist, a carelessly knotted black sarong rested on her hipbones.

'I'm not blowing things out of proportion. The fact is you've severely undermined me in the eyes of my colleagues.'

'Did it occur to you that singling you out for attention could be for a beneficial reason rather than a detrimental one?'

He couldn't breathe. And he couldn't move. Even though words emerged from his mouth, his tongue felt thick and all his blood was rushing painfully south. In exactly one minute, she'd know the effect she had on him.

The intensely crazy, intensely electrifying effect he'd thought he had under control.

Her mouth dropped open and her eyes widened. 'I…no, I didn't.'

His smile felt a little tight around the edges. 'Perhaps you should've given it a little further thought then. As for David and Cynthia, don't rule them out completely. They may be receiving phone calls as well. You may simply have been lucky number one, this time.' His gaze slid over her once more and he wondered how many other people had seen her in that bikini, her exquisite body on full show? He forced himself not to think about it.

She frowned. 'I find it hard to believe that you check on every single employee…' She stopped and took a breath. 'Ari, why did you really do it?'

The sound of his name on her lips sent hot lust-filled darts to his groin. 'Why does it upset you so much?' he murmured.

Her eyebrows shot up. 'Are you serious? I have to work with these people!'

He shrugged. 'Then I'll leave it in your capable hands to smooth things over, assure your colleagues that my HR director was conducting a simple employee assessment and you jumped to a conclusion. Because that's what really happened.'

'God, you really expect me to believe that, do you?'

'I do.'

'You must think I'm really gullible.'

'If I did, you wouldn't be working for me. And you shouldn't take too much stock in what others think of you. Unless that's the problem here? Are you saying you don't trust your own judgement, Perla?'

She froze. Before his eyes, her face leached all colour. Her fingers twisted around each other in a clearly distressed way that made him curse inwardly. 'Yes,' she whispered raggedly. 'That's exactly what I'm saying. I'm…I'm not a very good judge of character.'

The visible distress made something catch in his chest. Before he could think better of it, he closed the distance between them and took her chin in his hand. This close, the scent of her warm body mingled with the chlorine from her swim hit him in the throat. His blood pounded harder, but Ari consoled himself with the fact that with her gaze on his, she wasn't witnessing what her proximity was doing to him below the waist.

'What makes you think that?'

'I got it spectacularly wrong with you, didn't I?' she asked.

His mouth firmed. 'But I wasn't who you were thinking of just now.' He knew it as certainly as he knew his name.

'What, you read minds now?'

'No. But, unlike you, I can read people. Who was it, Perla?' he asked, although he had a fair idea.

'Does it take a genius to figure out that I misjudged the man I married?' she said, confirming his theory. 'I thought he was someone I could depend on. Instead, he…he…' She closed her eyes and shook her head. The pain in her face and her words struck a dark chord within him. A chord he absolutely did not want struck.

But he couldn't help it as memory gathered speed through his brain.

He'd grown up depending on his father, looking up to him, hanging on his every word. For most of his early years, he'd wanted nothing more than to follow in his father's footsteps, only to find out that they were the shoes of a philanderer, an extortionist and a fraudster. A man who would take his son's idolisation and attempt to use it against him…to manipulate it for his own selfish needs.

His gut tightened against the ragged pain he'd thought long buried but that seemed to catch him on the raw much too often these days. It didn't help his disposition to know that Perla was always present when it happened. That perhaps they shared a connection with hurt and betrayal.

'If you're talking about your husband, he was just one man. Don't let him cloud your judgement about everyone else. Trust your instincts.'

'*Trust my instincts?* I don't think that's a very good idea. My instincts told me *you* were a good guy. But you turned on me like I was some sort of criminal when you found out who I was.'

'I no longer think that, or you wouldn't be here.'

She opened her mouth to speak, paused, then eyed him. 'But that's only half true, isn't it? If you'd thought I could really cope on my own you wouldn't have stepped in.'

He dropped his hand, then immediately flexed it at his side when it continued to tingle wildly. 'You told me how long you'd been out of the corporate world. That, coupled with your husband's activities, placed you in a vulnerable position.'

'And you were trying to *save* me? How unnecessarily noble of you.' The hand she'd placed on her hips drew attention to her pert breasts. Breasts he'd feasted on for a long time that first night. Breasts he wanted to touch, to caress again more than he wanted his next breath.

He whirled away and focused on the views of the GW Monument and Capitol Hill in the distance, lit up beacons of power, hoping his brain would find a different focus other than replaying the sight of her in that pulse-destroying bikini.

'So, are you done berating me?' he asked. He wanted her gone before he did something completely stupid. Like finding out just how robust the wraparound sofa behind him would be with both their weights pounding it.

'No. I don't need saving, Ari.'

'Fine, I won't interfere. Even though you've clearly exacerbated a simple assessment directive, perhaps I should've just let things play out. Let's move on, shall we?'

Behind him, she heard her soft sigh. 'Move on. That's easy for you to say.'

His chest tightened. 'No, actually, it's not,' he said, then froze. *Where the hell had that come from?* Pushing his hands into his pockets, he hoped she would let the careless slip slide.

Instead, she came closer until she stood next to him. 'What do you mean?' she asked with a soft murmur.

He clenched his jaw for several seconds, then felt the words spiral out of him. 'It means I know what it feels like to be under scrutiny. To know that people are looking at you and forming judgements you have no control over. That at best you were being judged with pity and at worst with scorn and malice.'

She sucked in a shocked breath. 'God, who… why…?'

He turned and glanced at her. Her wide eyes were drowning in sympathy and her mouth was parted with agitation. The realisation that she wore that look for him struck him in the gut. 'You don't know about Alexandrou Pantelides, my father?'

She shook her head.

Giddy relief poured through him. 'Then I prefer to keep you in the dark just a little while longer.'

'Was he…was he the one you meant when you said *him* that day in your office?'

Another time, another slip. When it came to this woman, it seemed he didn't know when to shut the hell up. 'Yes,' he confessed.

'And you don't want to be like him? What did he do to you?' she asked, sympathy making her voice even huskier.

'Nothing I wish to share with you.'

Although a tinge of hurt washed over her eyes, she kept her gaze on him. 'Okay. But you know there's nothing to stop me from searching the Web for information the moment I leave here.'

His insides tightened at the thought of Perla knowing just how mired in deceit and humiliation his past was. 'No, there isn't. But it'll be an extra few minutes when I know you're not forming an opinion about me the way you think others are doing about you.'

'But if you know how it feels then why did you contact HR?'

'I saw a potential problem. I stepped in to fix it. It's what I do.' After his father had slashed their lives into a million useless pieces, seventeen-year-old Ari had assumed the role of protector. Protecting his mother and his younger brothers from the press intrusion after Alexandrou Pantelides's sleazy dealings and philandering lifestyle had come to light had, overnight, become his number-one priority.

His brothers, after severely rocky years, had grown into stable, intensely successful individuals. And his mother had eventually found peace. He'd believed his family was safe…

Until fate had shown him otherwise…

Theos, this was too much! Resentment that he'd inadvertently taken a trip down memory lane yet again coiled through him.

Sucking in a deep breath, he faced Perla. 'You've aired your grievance. I've listened. Now don't you have work to be getting on with?'

The harshness of his voice stung. 'It's my day off, but Ari—'

He let his gaze slide down her body, ignoring the fire sizzling through his veins. 'And was this what you meant when you suggested staying away from each other? Because this plan—' he indicated her skimpily clad form '—is a poor attempt at removing temptation from both our paths.'

'I'm sorry. I wasn't thinking… I just reacted—'

'Well, make a better judgement call next time!'

She flinched as if he'd struck her. But he couldn't regret his tone because he was drowning in hell. He'd almost opened up about secrets he shared with no one. And the temptation to unburden had been great. But not to her. Not to the woman whose husband had caused the media to dredge up all the bitterness and humiliation only a few short months ago.

He tightened his jaw and watched, fascinated, as she pulled herself together with a grace and dignity he found curiously admirable.

Crossing her arms round her middle, she glared at him. 'We're weak when it comes to each other. Striking out at me for your weakness is cowardly and beneath you. Stop it. Believe me, I can bite back.'

He felt a wash of heat surge up his cheekbones. 'You need to leave. Now. Before I do something we'll both regret.'

'Ari—'

'A word to the wise. No man likes being told he's weak; it can be misconstrued as a challenge. Leave. Now, Perla, before I invite you to honour your promise of biting me.'

Eyes wide, she backed quickly towards the door. 'We'll need to find a way of working together eventually, Ari.'

'Let's discuss it further when you're not wearing a whisper-thin sarong and a clinging bikini that's just *begging* to be ripped off.'

Perla tried not to count the ways things had gone spectacularly wrong as she left Ari's penthouse. First her headlong flight from the swimming pool, bristling with intense irritation and hurt, had been ill-timed. She should've waited to cool down before confronting him.

And what, in goodness' name, had she been thinking, going into his presence wearing two tiny pieces of Lycra and an even flimsier sarong?

But of all the things slamming through her

mind, it was the look on his face as he'd confessed that he'd walked in her shoes that struck deepest and made her kick herself for picking the wrong time to confront him.

His pain had been unmistakable. It was a different sort of pain from when he'd spoken about his wife but the dark torment had been present nonetheless.

Just how much had Arion Pantelides been through? And what the hell had his father done to him?

She reached her suite five floors below and immediately glanced at her laptop set atop the most exquisite console table. She dismissed the voice that whispered that knowledge was power. However foolish it might be, she couldn't forget the relieved look on Ari's face when she'd confessed to not knowing who his father was.

There'd been a point in time a few months ago when she would've given her right arm to remain oblivious to what Morgan had done.

If Ari craved privacy, she would grant him that.

As for his anger at the way she'd gone to him, dressed in only a bikini and a sarong... She glanced down and saw her body's visible reaction to him. Her nipples were sharp points of fierce need and the way her chest rose and fell in her agitation...

God, no wonder he'd been angry!

She sank onto her bed, overwhelmed by her body's turbulent response.

It was clear that staying away from each other the last three weeks had achieved none of the clarity and purpose they'd both sought. If anything, the attraction bit harder, the hunger sharper.

It was also clear that she'd overreacted to the HR director's call and possibly made her work situation worse.

But she was sure she hadn't imagined the cynical looks between her colleagues when all her suggestions on the various stages of the opening night for Pantelides WDC had been accepted without question. Pleased that she was being valued as a hard-working member, she'd put forward more suggestions.

It was why she'd begun questioning herself, and the call coming so close to that had made her storm from the rooftop pool with every intention of confronting Ari and taking him to task.

Of course it had nothing to do with the fact that she'd been unable to stop thinking about the man since Miami; she had found herself growing curiously bereft with his continued absence and the fact that her body seemed to have pulsed to life the moment she'd found out he was back.

She was here to do a job. She seriously needed to focus on that and nothing else.

Let's move on...

Pursing her lips, she pulled off her sarong. Ari was annoyingly right.

They had two weeks before this spectacular hotel set in the heart of America's political and cultural capital opened.

The hotel itself was a jaw-dropping architectural masterpiece, and fully expected to achieve six-star status within the next few weeks. They'd already hosted the industry critics, who'd since given glowing reviews.

With prime views of the Lincoln Memorial and Capitol Hill, the mid-twentieth-century building had been given a multi-million-dollar facelift that had seen it propelled to the realms of untold luxury and decadence.

Marble, slate and gleaming glass were softened by hues of eye-catching red-and-gold furniture and art that captured the imagination, and the five top-class restaurants were already booked well into the new year.

Regardless of her own shaky issues, Perla was hugely excited to be working on the hotel opening.

After showering and slipping on her bathrobe, she ordered room service and pulled open her laptop. Her research into the Washington scene had thrown up a few ideas for the opening. She'd already secured the jazz quartet said to be a favourite of the President to her list and confirmed the special tour of the Smithsonian and the White House for the VIP guests who would be staying overnight. Her idea of a midnight cruise on the Pantelides yacht had also been greeted with enthusiasm.

Feeling her confidence return, she pulled up the details of Oktoberfest on a whim, then immediately discarded it. Somehow she didn't think beer-drinking went well with Ari's vision for his hotel.

But there was nothing wrong with checking it out for herself while she was here. Something to do to take her mind off the fact that Ari was once again within seeing and touching distance…and the knowledge that her pulse skittered every time she admitted that fact.

Her doorbell ringing brought welcome relief from her thoughts. The scent of the grilled chicken and salad made her stomach growl and reminded her she hadn't eaten since a hastily snatched bagel and coffee first thing this morning.

Ravenous, she ate much faster than she should have, a fact she berated herself for when she bolted out of her chair, rushed to the bathroom and emptied the contents of her stomach a mere hour later.

'Are you all right? You look a bit peaky.'

Susan, the assistant concierge, peered at her as Perla waited for the list and notes she'd typed up last night to finish printing.

Perla nodded absently and smoothed her hand down her black skirt and matching silk shirt she'd worn for the meeting with Ari and the rest of the key hotel staff.

Glancing down at herself, she wondered if she'd made the right choice. The shirt hadn't felt this tight across the bust when she'd picked it as part of her work wardrobe a month ago. The gaping between the top buttons had forced her to leave the first and second buttons open and she questioned now whether she shouldn't have changed her outfit altogether.

But after waking up twice more to throw up, she'd eventually fallen into a deep sleep and missed her alarm.

Which was why she was hopelessly late—

'Do you intend to join us for this meeting, Perla?'

Ari stood behind her, tall, imposing, gorgeous beyond words. In the morning sun, the sprinkling of grey at his temples highlighted the sculpted perfection of his face. But it was his unique hazel eyes that made her belly spasm with heat and a whole load of lust.

'I…I was just coming.'

'Good to hear.' He turned on his heel and strode back into the conference room.

'Someone's got an armadillo in their bonnet,' Susan whispered, her eyes wide with speculation.

Perla grabbed the sheets, gave a non-committal smile to Susan and hurried across the marble floor in her three-inch heels, only to freeze when she entered the room.

The only seat left at the small conference table was next to Ari. She'd have to sit beside him, breathe in his spicy cologne, feel the warmth of him and place herself within his powerful aura for however long the blasted meeting took. Her throat dried as her heart rate roared.

Ari glanced up and sent her another impatient look, one that made her stash her unease and walk to his side.

Ideas for the opening event were discussed and tossed or kept as Ari saw fit. Half an hour later, he turned to her. 'Do you have your list?'

She nodded and passed copies around. 'The top four are secured. The other three are yet to be finalised...'

'*Oktoberfest?*' Ari demanded.

Perla frowned and glanced down at the sheet in her hand. 'Sorry, that wasn't supposed to be on there. It was an idea I thought of floating but I don't think it's the right image for this hotel.'

'You're right. It's not.'

Several of her colleagues exchanged glances. Perla ignored them. Pursing her lips, she met Ari's direct stare. 'Like I said, it wasn't supposed to be on the list—'

'But it would be perfect for the San Francisco hotel.' He put the list down and caught up a pen, flicking it through long, elegant fingers. 'Contact their concierge, tell them to trial it and give us feedback on how it goes. And make sure you take credit for it. As for the rest of the suggestions, I'm on board with the jazz quartet and the White House tour. Add it to the other maybes and we'll discuss a shortlist at the next meeting.'

Warmth oozed through her but her veins turned icy when she spotted the repeated exchanged glances. From the corner of her eye she saw Ari's jaw tighten as he brought the meeting to a close.

In her haste to leave his disturbing presence, she dropped her file. She retrieved it and straightened to find him blocking her path to the door.

Her heart jumped into her throat. 'Did you need something?'

His gaze drifted over her and he frowned. 'Is everything in your wardrobe black?'

'Excuse me?'

'Black doesn't suit you. It makes your skin look too pale.' His eyes dropped lower, the opening of her shirt.

She forced herself not to reach up and button her shirt. Or touch her skin to test if it really was on fire since his gaze burned her from the inside out. 'You stopped me from leaving to disparage my clothes?' She casually leaned against the table and lifted an eyebrow, although casual was the last thing she felt.

He rocked back on his heels and shoved his hands into his pockets. For several seconds he didn't speak. 'I see that I've made things difficult for you here,' he finally said.

The hint of contrition in his tone made her breath catch. Nonchalantly, she tried to shrug it away. 'It's partly my fault. I overreacted. I'll deal with it. As you said, I need to trust my instincts and my talent, and not what other people think.'

He nodded. 'Bravo,' he said. Thinking he would move out of her way, she started to take a step and paused when his mouth opened again. 'And if it doesn't earn me a sexual harassment charge, may I suggest you find a better fitting shirt that doesn't display all your assets?'

Her gasp echoed around the room. 'It's not that bad! And stop talking about my assets or I'll have to point out that shoving your hands in your pockets like that pulls your trousers across your junk and displays *your* assets. Not that I'm paying a lot of attention, of course,' she added hurriedly and felt her face flame.

God, she needed her head examined!

One eyebrow slowly lifted. 'Of course.' He remained planted in front of her, as if he had nothing better to do than to rile her.

Unable to stand his intense gaze, she glanced down and saw just how much cleavage she was displaying. *God!*

'I just…seem to have put on a little weight, that's all. And I was running a little late this morning so there was no time to change…' She grew restive beneath his continued silent scrutiny. 'Seriously, it's not that bad.'

His nostrils flared and a look passed through his eyes that made her think he was toying with the idea of arguing the point. Instead, he opened the door. 'After you,' he said.

Walking in front of him across the large marble foyer felt like walking the plank on some doomed pirate's ship. She was aware of the intensity of his scrutiny on her back, her legs…her bottom. Electricity sparked along her nerves and spread throughout her body.

Slowly she noticed the sound of last-minute preparations in the vast space had gradually faded as people stopped to stare.

David and Cynthia, the two colleagues who'd been recruited the same time as her, stood at the solid wood-carved reception, watching with blatant curiosity. She didn't need to turn around after she passed them to know they were whispering behind her back.

Same as she didn't need to turn around to notice the moment Ari veered off towards his own office. Because her skin stopped tingling and her pulse began to slow.

By the time she shut herself away in the tiny office behind the concierge's station, she was shaking. Going to her coffee stand, she flicked the kettle on and practised her breathing as it boiled. She poured water onto the tea bag, then immediately gagged as the scent of camomile made her stomach roil violently.

Abandoning tea in favour of water, Perla waited for the sickness to subside and threw herself into her work.

She spent the rest of the day finalising catering requirements, confirming bookings and chasing RSVPs. The turkey sandwich she ordered for lunch stayed put and she breathed a sigh of relief. The last thing she needed was to get sick within the first month of starting a new job in which she already felt compromised.

But by six o'clock her feet ached, her head throbbed with a dull ache and the debilitating weakness that had dogged her all day was weighting her limbs. Shutting off her computer, she dug through her bag and located the painkillers she always kept to hand. Swallowing two, she took the lift to her suite, collapsed onto the bed, kicked off her shoes and pulled the covers over her head.

The buzzing of her phone woke her an hour later.

Dazed, she pushed the hair off her face and snagged the handset. 'Hello?'

'Perla.'

Excitement jack-knifed through her body.

God, the way he said her name should be banned. Or she needed to charge for it. Because she was sure she suffered a tiny nervous breakdown every time his voice grated out her name like that.

'Um…hi,' she mumbled, squinting in the darkened room.

'Did I wake you?' There was a frown in his voice.

'No, I was just…no.'

'I've been thinking about your predicament.'

'What predica…? No, I told you, I'll handle it.'

'You may not need to. Have you had dinner yet?' he asked.

She tried to make her brain work. 'No, I haven't.'

'Meet me at the Athena Restaurant in half an hour,' he said, naming the five-star restaurant on the first floor of the Pantelides WDC, headed by a very sought after Michelin-starred chef.

Perla flicked the bedside lamp on and struggled to sit up. Thankfully, her headache seemed to have disappeared. 'Um…why?'

'I have a proposal to discuss with you. A new opportunity you might be interested in.'

The thought of meeting with Ari so openly again after this morning and being the cynosure of all eyes made her nape tighten. Exhaling, she faced up to the fact she had to deal with that sooner or later. She refused to let gossip rock the self-esteem she was trying hard to rebuild.

She cleared her throat. 'I'd love to hear your proposal but I think the Athena is fully booked tonight. And yes, I know you own the hotel and can chuck someone out but I'd feel bad. Do you think we can order room service instead?'

For a few seconds, silence greeted her suggestion. 'Given our track record, do you think being in a hotel room alone together is wise?' he rasped.

Liquid heat flooded her belly, followed closely by chagrin. 'Um, you're right, it's not. I'll…come to you.'

'Half an hour. Don't keep me waiting.'

She hung up and threw the covers off. Going to the bathroom, she took a quick shower, pleased that she felt a whole lot better now than she had all day.

The dress she chose was functional and stylishly respectable without being overtly sexy. Pulling on the slingbacks she'd discarded earlier, she caught up her black clutch and black wrap and left her room.

Despite telling herself this was just business, butterflies fluttered madly in her stomach as the lift rushed her downward.

She stepped out of the lift and was about to head towards the foyer when her phone pinged.

Come outside. A

Slowly, she swivelled on her heels and headed out into the cool October night. Beneath the elegantly columned portico of the hotel, Ari leaned, cross-legged and cross-armed against a gleaming black sports car.

The sight of him, magnificently imposing, arrestingly gorgeous, was incredibly dangerous to her well-being. He wore a dark blue cotton shirt with black trousers and a matching jacket that hugged his wide shoulders.

The intensity of his stare as it drifted over her made her body grow hot all over. And even though he didn't say anything, by the time his gaze returned to hers she had the distinct impression he was displeased.

But then what else was new? Ari alternated between finding her irritating and being incredibly considerate.

Given the choice, I'd settle for a little bit of peace.

'What did you say?' he asked, straightening from the car to open the passenger door for her.

Realising she'd muttered her thoughts, she blushed. 'Nothing. I thought we were meeting inside?'

He shook his head. 'Change of plan. I thought we could experience what Washington DC has to offer. You had a Greek restaurant on your list. Care to try it?' he asked.

Pleased that he'd remembered, she smiled. 'I'd love to.'

He straightened, waited for her to slide in and shut the door behind her.

Unable to stop herself, Perla watched him round the bonnet. God, even the way this man moved demanded attention. His lean, sinewy grace seemed innate.

The moment he shut the door all her senses flared to life. His scent was intoxicating, addictive in a way that made her want to throw herself across the console and slide her greedy hands all over him.

Expecting him to start the car and drive, she glanced at him and caught his rigid profile. When his fingers wrapped around the steering wheel and gripped tight, she knew he was fighting the same raw need.

She must have made a sound because a choked noise filled the tense space.

'Ari…'

He sucked in a jagged breath. 'We are not teenagers and we are not animals.' His voice was rough, darkly husky. 'We have enough self-control to be able to resist this…this *insanity* between us.'

Her hand tightened around her clutch. 'I agree.' Although fighting it felt like a losing battle right now.

'What happened between us can't happen again,' he continued gratingly. The mild self-loathing in his voice finally pierced the cocoon of sensual delirium.

Stung, she whipped her head to stare out of her window. 'I get the message loud and clear, Ari.'

'Do you?' he demanded, and she knew he was

staring at her because she could feel the intensity of his gaze on her skin.

She bit her lip to stop another helpless moan from escaping. 'You hate me because I remind you of something in your past. I don't know what exactly. Maybe it's connected to this insane temptation we can't kill. I could find a reason to hate you too but what good would hate do either of us?'

'I don't hate you,' he growled. 'There are a lot of things I feel but, rest assured, *hate* isn't one of them.'

A little bit of the hurt eased but hearing that self-loathing still present in his voice made her heart lurch. 'That's good to hear.' She took a deep breath and immediately regretted it when his scent filled every atom of her being. 'I'd suggest handing in my notice and finding a new job if I could—' She jumped at the snarl that filled the car. 'But I've only been working a few weeks, and my chances of finding another job are—'

'You're not quitting this job. You're not going anywhere.' He pressed the button that started the ignition but he didn't drive away. 'You signed a contract so you're staying put.'

CHAPTER EIGHT

ARI MADE SURE his words left no room for doubt or ambiguity. Which was laughable, considering he was nowhere near as stalwart under the barrage of the emotions coursing through him.

He'd firmly believed he had regained some control after yesterday's incident. It was the reason he'd called to discuss business with her. He'd been so certain, after seeing her in that bikini and not jumping on her like some hormone-riddled teenager, he could see Perla, be within touching distance of her without experiencing that unbridled depth of yearning that seemed to claw up from his very soul.

A soul he'd believed withered and charred after Sofia…after his father…

But now, with her seductive, addictive warmth so close, her husky voice seeming to caress him whenever she spoke, he knew resisting this insanity wouldn't be as easy as he'd thought.

But resist he had to. The guilt that had ridden him from the very moment he'd slept with

Perla still resided beneath his chest. It fought savagely with his intense attraction but it never went away…

I remind you of something in your past…

She had no idea how accurate that was.

'Okay, I'll honour my contract. But, um…do you think we can get out of here? The valet attendants are beginning to get frantic at the backed-up traffic.'

A quick look in the rear-view mirror confirmed her words. With a twist of the wheel and a foot on the accelerator, he squealed out of his hotel's driveway and onto the freeway. The sound of the throaty engine drowned out his thoughts for the precious few seconds it took to regain a little bit of his control.

Masculine pleasure at the purr of the powerful engine beneath him soothed his turbulent pulse and he inhaled slowly.

Next to rowing, alone or with his brothers, powerful engines like these were his passion. Except he didn't get to indulge enough. It was probably why he'd succumbed to temptation—

Stasi! Enough with the excuses. Perla had hit the nail on the head. They'd been weak with temptation and he'd succumbed. Not once but twice. The only way to avoid being no better than his father would be to make sure it didn't happen again.

'Ari, could you slow down a little, please?'

A quick glance showed her death grip on the

bucket seat. He cursed under his breath and eased off the pedal. 'My apologies.'

She nodded and her fingers relaxed. 'What did you want to talk to me about?' she asked as he signalled off Connecticut Avenue and slid to a stop in front of the Greek restaurant. Perla didn't know it but it was one of his favourite restaurants outside of his homeland.

As they were led in, he found himself following the line of her body again. The way her black dress hugged her tight behind, the way her black wrap caressed her shoulders and her black heels made her legs go on for ever.

His thoughts screeched to a halt. She was wearing black again. And not just a touch here and there but black from head to toe…as if she was making a statement.

Was she?

'You're scowling again.'

They'd reached their table and she was already sitting down, while he stood beside it, arrested by his crazy thoughts. He gritted his teeth, pulled out his chair and sat down.

Business. Focus on business.

'You asked what I wanted to talk to you about.'

She nodded as he beckoned the *sommelier*. She ordered a white wine spritzer and he a full-bodied claret. Once they were alone again, he took out his mini tablet and set it on the table between them. A few swipes and he had the page he was looking for.

'My new resort and casino in Bermuda, set to open in two months.'

Her brow rose. 'Another one?' She leaned closer and swiped through the pictures. Slowly her mouth fell open. 'It's spectacular.'

He allowed himself a small smile. 'I worked closely with the architects to achieve the results I wanted—a private resort which caters to extreme water sports lovers without taking anything away from the signature luxury casino.'

'Water seems to be a major theme for you, doesn't it? Eighty per cent of your portfolio is built on or around water.'

He was impressed that she'd done her homework. 'I grew up around water and started rowing from a very early age.'

'You rowed?' she asked in surprise.

'Competitively for six years, four of those with Sakis and two with Theo.' It had been one of the few ways he and his brothers had coped with their shattered lives.

She played with the beads on her purse. 'Did you win?'

'Of course.'

She laughed, the sound so pure and delightful, his stomach clenched. '*Of course*. How many titles?'

'Five that are worth mentioning. My mother has all my trophies from when I was a child.'

Her head tilted to one side, traces of laughter lingering in her eyes. 'I can't quite picture you as a child. You look as if you were born looking like you do now.'

Against his will, his smile widened. 'For my mother's sake, I'm glad that wasn't the case.'

A sudden wave of anguish passed over her face, erasing the laughter. Then it was gone. Reaching out, she took a slice of bread from the basket the waiter had set between them and broke off a piece. 'Is your mother still around?'

He tried not to let his mixed feelings about his mother show. 'Yes. She lives at the family home in Athens.'

Curiosity built in her eyes. 'Do you see her often?'

He shrugged. 'When I'm in Greece. Which isn't often enough, she tells me.'

'Are you two close?' He detected the faint longing in her voice and wondered at it. It suddenly struck him that, beyond the intense sexual pull and the actions of her dead husband, he didn't know much about Perla Lowell.

'We used to be. There was a time when I shared everything with her. She was my best friend and she encouraged my every dream. Then...my father happened.'

Her breath caught slightly. 'He...*happened?*'

The usual fierce reluctance to revisit the past spiked through him, even though he'd been the one to open the door. Despite his reticence, he found himself nodding. 'A few months before I turned eighteen, a journalist uncovered my father's duplicitous life. Details of fraud, corruption, embezzlement all came to light.' His insides twisted with remembered agony that he hoped his face didn't reflect. 'Overnight, our lives were turned upside down. I was working in one of my father's companies and was in the office with my father when the fraud squad stormed the building.'

Her eyes widened. 'That must have been very difficult to witness.'

'It would've been if I hadn't realised quickly that I would be busy trying to save my own skin.'

'*What?* Why?'

For a moment, he considered not uttering the words. Considered hiding it from her the way he'd hidden this fact from his brothers, from his mother. Only a distant uncle knew what Ari had suffered, and Ari had made sure to enforce the attorney-client privilege that prevented his uncle from ever divulging the truth.

'My father tried to shift some of the blame of his fraudulent activities onto me. He implicated me in a few of his bribery scams and tried to get me to take the fall so his charges could be lessened.'

Her eyes darkened with shock. 'Oh, God! Why would he do that?'

'I was his firstborn son, and had taken a keen interest in the business since I turned sixteen. I had a good head for figures and the authorities knew he'd been grooming me to eventually take over from him. Because I was still under eighteen when he was arrested he figured I would get off easily. For a short while the authorities believed him.'

Her eyes grew dark with sympathy. 'That's horrible. How did your brothers take it? Where was your mother?'

Unable to stop, his lips twisted as old wounds were ripped open. 'Sakis and Theo didn't know... I never told them.'

Her mouth dropped open. 'You didn't?'

He shrugged. 'What good would it have done? By the time we were done with my father, enough devastation had been spread around. It was my duty to protect them from more hurt. Revealing that I possibly faced jail when they were counting on me was not an option.'

'But...you've been carrying it for all this time...'

'Human beings are predisposed to carrying a hell of a lot of baggage,' he answered. 'And I have very broad shoulders,' he added, in the hope of lightening a suddenly heavy atmosphere. But her eyes only grew more solemn, as if she shared his pain, sympathised with his blighted past.

'Broad shoulders or not, you shouldn't have had to bear that on your own. Your mother…'

'Retreated to our villa in Santorini and locked herself away. Her husband's betrayal was too much for her. She couldn't cope.' He'd needed her more than ever in the darkest time of his life. And she'd abandoned him. Just as she'd abandoned Sakis and Theo when they'd needed her the most.

It had taken a long time for Ari to forgive her, a long time to get past his anger and bitterness at her weakness. But he'd learned to smother it. Because he'd needed to get past his personal devastation in order to take care of his brothers. To salvage the charred remains of the family business his father had decimated with his greed and carelessness.

He jerked as Perla's hand touched his in gentle sympathy. 'I'm sorry that happened to you.'

Sincerity blazed from her clear green eyes. Sincerity he wanted to take and wrap around his damaged heart. Instead, he forced himself to nod.

Slowly, he pulled his hand away.

Because, even in the midst of excruciating reminiscing, he could feel that pull again, that potent hunger that lurked like the sweetest siren call, ready to tempt him.

'Why?'

Her fingers curled around her piece of bread.

'Because…because no one deserves to go through what you did.'

Their drinks arrived and he took a healthy gulp of wine, exhaling in satisfaction as the fire in the alcohol temporarily replaced the fire of lust. 'But I survived. Some would say I triumphed.'

'But you're still affected by it, aren't you?'

He tensed. 'Excuse me?'

'Yesterday you didn't want me to find out what your father had done. Clearly you're still affected by what happened.'

'Are we not all shaped by our pasts to some extent? You're clearly steeped in the past and reacting to your own experiences.'

Her cheeks lost a bit of colour. 'What makes you say that?'

'Yesterday *you* admitted your lack of judgement when it comes to dealing with people. I don't need to be a genius to work out the root cause of it.'

Paling further, she shook her head. 'I…I'm not…'

'Tell me how you met Lowell?' he asked before he could stop himself. 'Of all the men you could've dated, why him?'

'Because I didn't have a crystal ball that could look into the future to see how things would turn out. And you say *of all the men* as if I had hundreds at my feet.'

He barely stopped himself from glancing up at her hair. The idea that no man had shown interest in her was laughable. 'So he was the first man to show his interest?' He tried to force a neutral tone and barely pulled it off.

'He was charming; he paid me the right sort of attention…at the beginning. I believed I was making the right choice, that we had the same goals and that my feelings were reciprocated.'

Anger roiled through his belly. 'Instead, he abandoned you shortly after you were married?'

Shocked eyes met his. 'How did you know that?'

'I'm a major shareholder in the company he tried to destroy. My brother dealt with the bulk of the investigation but I saw enough.'

Her gaze grew haunted, then it slid away and she reached for the glass of water. After a few sips she set the glass down. 'So you know a great deal about me.'

'Enough to know there are no mention of your parents anywhere on record. You take care of your in-laws but what about your own parents?' he asked, eager to get away from the subject of dead spouses.

The earlier anguish he'd glimpsed returned. 'I don't have… I was placed in the foster system when I was one month old. My birth mother left me in front of the social security office with my first name and my date of birth pinned to my blanket. My birth date could be wrong because there was no birth certificate, although the doctors are fairly sure I was born in the month I was left but there were no hospital records so I don't even know *where* I was born. So no, I have no record of who my parents are,' she murmured in a voice ravaged with pain. 'I'm the child no one wanted.'

His fingers tightened around his glass and he realised he was holding on tight so he wouldn't reach out for her like she'd reached out for him.

Only he wanted to take her face between his hands and kiss away her pain. He wanted to re-wind time, take a different track of conversation that was so far off what he'd come here for it was ludicrous. He should've stuck to business, facts, figures.

Not their painful personal pasts. And he should certainly not be sitting here, hanging onto that connection that stemmed from opening up and sharing his desolate history with her.

He wasn't a *sharer*.

'Perla—'

She forced a laugh. 'How do we always end up on the personal when we vow never to again?'

'We're especially bad at pulling the forbidden out of each other.'

'Or exceptionally good?' she joked.

He stared at her. And just like that the mad-ness descended again. He tried to shift away from it but it clawed into him, sank its merciless tal-ons into his gut and held him down. Almost in slow motion, he watched her mouth part, her nostrils quiver delicately as she sucked in a desperate breath.

Theos!

She gave a distressed shake of her head and glanced down at the now powered down tablet. 'The resort. We were discussing the resort,' she said after clearing her throat.

He forced his mind on track. 'Yes. I wanted to float the idea of you handling the pre-opening VIP events for the Bermuda resort on your own. If you agree to take on the task, you'll have to work fast to organise it. The guests arrive at the resort at the end of next week.'

'The pre-opening event is so your A-list clients can experience the resort and spread the word to their other A-list friends by the time the resort opens properly, correct?'

He nodded. 'So it needs to be extra-special. Your input here in Washington has been invaluable and you can choose to stay here if you wish, but I think this is more along the lines of what you used to do in your previous position, only on a much larger scale?'

'Yes, but I've never worked in such an exotic location before.'

'This will be your chance to prove yourself then. I want to see how you fare spearheading a larger project.' He sipped his wine—absently acknowledging he would have to abandon his beloved sports car in favour of another means of transport to return to the hotel—and watched her digest the information.

Slowly her stunning green eyes widened. '*Spearheading?* Are you serious?'

'You can handpick your own team, hire and fire as you see fit. You'll be provided with the initial list of attending guests but you can extend the list if you think you can handle it.'

'You *are* serious!' Shocked happiness erased the last evidence of her bleak foray into the past and, watching her, enchantment eased through him.

Examining himself closer, he realised he felt lighter than he had in a long while. He refused to believe unburdening his past to Perla had succeeded in lightening the heavy load of bitterness and pain, but he had no other explanation for it.

When he found himself smiling in reaction to her still stunned expression, something tugged hard in his chest. 'Serious enough to promise a quick firing and slow roasting if you mess up my opening.'

She popped another piece of bread into her mouth. 'Which is really no better than a slow firing and a quick roasting since both sound horrific.'

He laughed and saw her gaze linger on his face and her eyes darken a fraction.

No, he wasn't going there. *They* were not going there.

He beckoned the hovering waiter and paused as Perla examined the menu. Slowly she pulled her lower lip into her mouth and pondered some more.

'Can I help?' he offered after several minutes.

She looked up in relief. 'Would you? I never know what to order when I go to a restaurant and I always end up hating what I choose and coveting what's on other people's plates.'

'I'll order a variety of dishes and you can decide which ones you like and which ones you don't.'

She smiled. 'That works for me. *Efharisto.*'

He froze, the sound of his mother tongue so erotically charged coming from her that he forgot to breathe. 'You're learning Greek?'

'I work for a Greek company. It seems wise to learn a few essential words like *thank you* and *where the hell is the coffee?* I find some of the pronunciations quite hard, though.'

'Let me know what you have difficulty with and I'll teach you.' Again the words slipped out before he could stop them.

What in heaven's name was wrong with him?

Mentally shaking his head, he recited the dishes he wanted prepared to the waiter and added a command for haste.

They discussed the Bermuda resort and her initial ideas. The passion she exhibited for business made him glad he'd offered her the chance. So much so, he slightly regretted it when their meal arrived and intruded on the atmosphere. Small platters of roasted vegetables, tenderly prepared meats served on a bed of traditional salad, hummus and oven-baked breads.

He watched her dig into the food with the same gusto she'd eaten that night at his apartment in London. Then, as now, he'd found her appetite refreshing.

Recalling her comment earlier about putting on weight, Ari's gaze slid to her breasts. They looked slightly heavier, plumper than they had in London, and her cleavage seemed deeper.

Warmth rushed into his mouth that had nothing to do with the sumptuous textures of the food and everything to do with recalling the exquisite taste of her hard nipples on his tongue. He forced his gaze away. Only to snap it back to her when she made a sound of distress.

Her eyes had widened and she was reaching for her water. 'Um…Ari…I don't feel so good.'

Ari frowned and he jerked to his feet. 'What's wrong? What is it?'

She dropped her glass and water splashed across the table. In one move, he was by her side, pushing her chair back so he could take her face in his hands.

'Perla?'

She jumped up and looked around wildly, drawing the attention of other diners. She must have spotted the signs for the lavatory because she grabbed her bag and lurched forward.

'Excuse me.' She clamped her hand over her mouth and fled.

CHAPTER NINE

THE DEBILITATING WEAKNESS was back again, weighting her limbs down and fanning a dull ache throughout her body.

But it was nothing compared to the crushing weight of suspicion anchoring her heart.

No matter how much she tried to push the thought away, it kept coming back, intruding, demanding to be heard, to be acknowledged.

Perla cast a furtive glance at the man who stood beside her in the hotel lift, his hand gripping her arm. He hadn't said a word since they left the restaurant. He'd been there when she emerged from the Ladies, pale, weak and shaky, barely able to meet his gaze when he'd enquired whether she wanted to leave.

The restaurant staff had been profusely apologetic but she hadn't had the courage to reassure them that what was going on was most likely not the fault of their food. She'd left the soothing of ruffled feathers to Ari, simply because she hadn't been able to think past the stark reality of what she could be facing.

They exited the lift and she followed him numbly. It wasn't until they were inside the suite that was easily three times the size of hers that she realised they hadn't returned to her suite but to his. He bypassed the living room, the study and the master bedroom and entered a second bedroom.

Before her stood what was easily an emperor-sized bed, complete with solid four-posters and cream silk muslin curtains. A bathroom and walk-in closet were visible through a golden-lit arch and beyond the windows Washington DC shone its powerful light over the city.

Her gaze returned from sweeping the room to find Ari standing with his hands on his hips, those mesmerising eyes fixed questioningly on hers.

'There's a new toothbrush through there if you need to use it?'

She nodded, dropped her clutch on the bed and darted into the bathroom. The need to escape was less to do with cleaning her mouth properly and more to do with delaying the inevitable.

Quickly, she brushed her teeth and rinsed her mouth. Then gripped the edge of the sink as a fresh wave of apprehension rolled through her.

Arion Pantelides wasn't stupid. The knowledge in his eyes told her his thoughts had taken the same path as hers.

'Perla.'

She jumped and whirled so fast, her vision blurred.

Callused hands steadied her, one curving around her waist and the other rising to cradle her cheek for a moment before he dropped his hand.

'Come.'

The gentle gesture threatened her equilibrium and she fought not to react as he led her back to the room and sank onto the bed beside her. He'd discarded his jacket and folded back the sleeves of his shirt.

The sight of the silky hairs on his forearm made sensation scythe through her but it was the look in his eyes that stopped her breath.

His fingers trembled as they caught her chin and an emotion moved through her heart she was almost too afraid to examine. 'How do you feel?' he asked in a low, deep voice.

Something in his tone made her glance at him. His face had lost a few shades of vibrancy and in his eyes dark, unfathomable shadows lurked.

Whatever was ahead of them, Perla knew it wouldn't be an easy road.

'I...I'm...' Her throat felt swollen and scratchy so she stopped.

'Here, have some water.' He passed her a glass and waited while she took a few sips. His gaze never left her and, feeling her hands begin to shake, she put the glass down.

Trepidation welled up inside her. 'Ari…'

More colour leached from his face. 'Before you say anything, Perla, I need you to be one hundred per cent sure.'

The depth of emotion in his voice made her heart flip over, then thunder with enough force to threaten her ribs. 'Why?' she asked before she could stop herself.

'Because the ramifications would mean more than you could ever imagine.' The roughness in his voice and the faint trembling of the hand still at her waist made her insides quake.

Incomprehensible emotions swirled around inside her. Unbidden, tears welled up in her eyes and slipped down her cheeks.

'*Theos*, do not cry. Please,' he ordered raggedly.

'Sorry, I'm not normally a crier,' she muttered, then cringed as more tears fell. 'I just can't seem to help myself.'

He gritted his teeth and brushed her cheeks with his thumbs, then stared down at her with dark eyes but said nothing as the tears continued to fall.

The knock on the door made him turn away but not before she caught another glimpse of jagged torment in his eyes. 'The doctor's here.'

'The *doctor?*' When had he even called him? 'Ari, I don't need a doctor. I feel fine.'

He stood and stared at her for a long moment before he shoved his hands into his pockets. 'I can send him away if that's what you want. But I think we need to make absolutely sure that you're not coming down with an illness. *That* is not negotiable. So we can do it now or we can do it tomorrow. Your choice.'

She gripped the covers, the feeling of hurtling towards the unknown growing by the second. But Ari was right. They needed to be sure nothing else was wrong before they went any further.

She nodded. 'Okay, we do it now.'

He left the room and returned moments later followed by a tall, lanky man with brown hair and serious brown eyes. He proceeded to look her over and fire questions at her that made her cringe. Ari stood, hand in his pocket next to the bed the whole time, his eyes never leaving her.

'The headache and fatigue worries me a bit, and your glands are slightly swollen,' the doctor finally said. 'My advice is to rest for a few days—'

'Yes, she'll do that—'

'No, she won't,' she countered sharply with a frown which he returned twice as hard and twice as dangerous. 'I'm not sick, Ari. Seriously, I'll be fine by morning.'

The doctor looked between them, clearly sensing the undercurrents. 'Or I can give you a flu shot just in case? Head it off at the pass?'

At her nod, he opened his bag and took out the needle. She tensed and tried to curb her nerves but Ari's narrowed gaze told her he'd seen her reaction.

Rounding the bed, he slid in beside her and pulled her close, his warm, hard body a solid comfort. 'You fear needles and yet you're refusing the simple alternative.'

'I'll take a small prick any day compared to days lazing about in bed.'

The small charged silence that followed gave her time to hear her words echo in the room. Then a fierce blush washed over her face.

The doctor hid a smile as he focused on preparing the syringe. Ari's mocking laughter lightened the tense atmosphere a touch, although she could feel his tension. 'It's not gentlemanly to laugh at a harmless *double entendre*. Especially when it comes at the patient's expense.'

He blinked and his gaze dropped to her mouth.

This close, his designer stubble was within touching distance and the gold flecks in his eyes and the sensual curve of his mouth were even more mesmerising. The hand he'd slipped around her tightened, drawing her infinitesimally closer to his body. Heat oozed through her, breaking loose that wild yearning she seemed to be useless at keeping sealed up.

The doctor clearing his throat made her jump. The needle filled with liquid was poised against her skin. 'Stop! Will this harm a pregnancy?' she blurted.

Beside her, Ari tensed.

The doctor frowned. 'Are you pregnant, Miss Lowell?'

'It's Mrs…actually,' she murmured absently as her gaze swung and collided with Ari's. In that moment, she *knew*.

And so did he.

The doctor moved. With a swiftness that stunned the breath out of her, Ari grabbed the doctor's needle-holding hand and held it in a death grip. All without taking his eyes from hers.

'So you're sure?' he rasped.

She nodded.

Wordlessly he let go of the doctor's wrist. Lines of torment bracketed his mouth as he left the bed.

She was pregnant. With Ari's child. The two thoughts tumbled over one another in her brain, one seeking dominance over the other and neither coming out the victor. Because both thoughts were equally mind-boggling.

Vaguely, she heard him dismiss the doctor and leave the suite.

But all too soon he was back. Tall, imposing, bristling with emotions she was too cowardly to try and name.

For several minutes, he paced the room. Then he finally stopped at the foot of the bed. 'Did you know you were pregnant?' His voice was gritty with emotion.

'No, I didn't. I didn't even guess.'

'Not even when you were late? How late are you?'

The date flared like a beacon in her mind. 'Almost two weeks.'

He muttered a word she didn't need translation for. '*Theos!*' Running a hand through his hair, he resumed pacing. 'And it didn't raise any alarms?'

'No. My period has always been irregular.'

She thought back to that night and felt shame crawl over her skin when she remembered she'd been so into it, too far gone with delirium that she hadn't stopped to think about safe sex that second time.

And now she was pregnant.

Tiny waves of joy slowly spread through her stunned senses.

A child of her own. To cherish and love. And, if she was lucky, a child who would love her back.

She jerked upright, her hand rushing to cover her stomach. 'Oh, God, I took some painkillers this afternoon!'

His gaze sharpened on her. 'What did you take?'

She told him. 'W…would it have harmed the baby?'

He shook his head. 'The doctor told me which medicines are okay to take during pregnancy.'

Relief poured through her. 'You asked him?'

Ari stilled. 'Of course. This baby is mine too,' he grated out.

But it didn't take a genius to see that he wasn't thrilled about it. Pain and hurt scythed through her joy. A second later a rush of protectiveness enveloped her.

'I realise this is unexpected. I don't want you to think that you need to be involved in any way...'

'Excuse me?' His voice was a rasp, his eyes dark with thunder as he stared at her.

Perla licked her lips, contemplated taking a sip of water and discarded the idea. She was too shaken not to pour it all over herself.

'I mean this wasn't planned or anything, so don't feel as if you have to participate in any decision-making. I'll take care of it.'

'You'll *take care of it?*'

The skin-flaying fury in his voice made her realise that once again she'd chosen the wrong words.

'No! I meant I'll take care of him or her after the birth.'

Dark implacable eyes bored into hers. 'So, just so we're clear, you intend to keep the baby?'

'Of course! I'd never, ever dream of...' She raised her chin. 'Yes, I intend to have this baby. What I meant was that I'll take sole responsibility so you don't have to worry.' Her eyes dropped to her stomach. This child was hers and she intended to protect him or her with her last breath.

'What gives you the right to assume sole responsibility for the child? Sexual responsibility is a two-way street.'

'I know, but I participated too without giving a thought to protection. Arion, all I'm trying to say is there's no need to get all macho and blame yourself for something that involved both of us.'

'Perla, look at me.' The order was soft, deadly.

She dragged her eyes from where she'd been staring at her stomach in silent wonder. The resolution and implacable determination in his eyes made her shiver.

'Do I look like the sort of man who would leave his child to be brought up by another man? And I assume you don't intend to remain single for the rest of your life? That you will seek another relationship at some point in the future?'

That thought was so unlikely she wanted to laugh. Except the look on his face told her he wouldn't find it funny. So she shrugged. 'I don't know. Maybe.'

'Let's try something else much simpler.' He drew closer to the bed. His hands hung loose at his sides and his open-legged stance was unthreatening. But she didn't fool herself for one second that Ari wasn't seething beneath that calm exterior. 'Do I look like I'm going anywhere?'

'Ari—'

'*Do I?*'

'No. You don't.' And she wasn't sure whether to be pleased or frightened by that admission.

If Ari wanted this child and, from his stance, she concluded he did…for now…it would mean she would have him in her life for the foreseeable future.

Her childhood in foster care had opened her eyes to the fact that not all children were wanted. No matter what the circumstances of conception, there came a point in time where some parents simply abandoned their children and walked away.

She had no intention of ever doing that to her child. But she couldn't speak for Ari. His childhood had created deep scars that rippled through his every decision. He'd been let down by the people who should've been there for him. In a way it was worse than never having felt the love of two devoted parents. She hadn't experienced that particular devastation because she hadn't had the fantasy in the first place. To know that he'd had parents who'd let him down, who'd let him shoulder the responsibility of caring for his brothers on his own was too distressing to bear.

A wave of despair swept over her. Would Ari let go of his pain long enough to let himself love a child?

'Good, I'm glad we've established that fact.' He stepped back from the bed and turned towards the door. Without speaking another word, he left.

He returned less than ten minutes later with a tray of food which he set on her lap. The simple ham and cucumber sandwich made her stomach rumble and she remembered she'd barely eaten a few mouthfuls of dinner before her attack.

'I prepared it myself. Until I find you a personal chef who will be apprised of all your dietary requirements, I'll prepare all your meals myself.'

Her mouth dropped open for several seconds before she managed to snap it shut. 'Wait... What?'

He poured a glass of orange juice and handed it to her. 'Which part needs explanation?'

'The part...all of it. You don't have to do this, Ari.'

'Yes, I do. You're carrying my child. I absolutely have to do this.'

Again, the depth of emotion behind the words made her eyes widen. But when she looked at him, his eyes were veiled and his face inscrutable.

'Eat,' he instructed.

In silence she ate because as much as she wanted to argue with him, probe behind his words, she was starving. And she needed to do everything in her power to keep her baby healthy and safe.

She forced herself to eat slowly this time. She accepted a second glass of orange juice. Once she'd drained it, Ari set the tray aside.

'How do you feel?' Again there was that concern in his voice. But, coupled with that, there was a thin vein of anxiety that made her heart skitter.

'I'm fine. Right now I'm more interested in how *you* feel.'

He rose with the tray. 'My feelings are irrelevant. Get some sleep. We'll talk in the morning.'

She wanted to ask what exactly they would be talking about, but he was already leaving, his shoulders and back set in tense lines that made her nervousness rise higher.

Her hand slid down to rest on her abdomen.

Whatever it was, she could handle it. As long as it didn't interfere with the welfare of her baby.

He was having a child.

Ari barely managed to set the tray down before it slid out of his useless grip.

Shaking from head to toe, he gripped the edge of the granite counter in the suite's kitchen and tried to breathe.

He was having a child!

The self-indulgent need to rail at fate was so strong the growl bubbled up through his chest before he managed to swallow it down. He stalked to the living room and contented himself with a fiery shot of single malt Scotch. Except he was no better equipped to handle the bone-crushing fear gripping him. It writhed like a poisonous snake inside him before sinking its merciless fangs into his heart.

Was he doomed to fail at this task too, the way he'd failed Sofia? He'd single-handedly taken care of his brothers and his mother, had ensured they were protected as much as possible from the fall-out of his father's misdeeds.

And yet he hadn't been able to save his wife.

Or his unborn child.

Was fate taunting him again? Willing him to fail again?

No!

His fist tightened around the glass and he set it aside before it shattered. This time things would be different. Because anything else was unthinkable.

He moved restlessly across the room, willing his pulse to slow, his insides to stop churning viciously with the acrid mix of guilt and fear.

He was going to be a father. His steps slowed and he stopped in front of the view. Funny, he'd stood here just two days ago thinking he was in control of his world. It had been in the moments before Perla burst in and accused him of controlling her life.

Now he barely felt in control of his.

Whirling round, he walked out of the living room and entered his study. It might be the middle of the night in Washington, but it was still a working day in London and the rest of Europe.

His first call was to the Pantelides headquarters in London, where he gathered all the pertinent information he needed. Next he placed a call to his lawyers in Greece. His dealings with them so far had been purely business so he wasn't surprised at their thinly veiled shock as he outlined his wishes.

By the time he finished his calls, the horizon was lightening with the coming dawn.

Ari rubbed a hand across his jaw and rested his head against his seat.

He had no idea how Perla would take the conversation he intended to have with her come morning. There could potentially be many obstacles to getting his way but he intended to smash them all aside.

Because one thing had become clear in his mind from the second he'd found out Perla was carrying his child.

The welfare of his child was the most important thing in his life.

She was already up when he knocked on her door just after seven o'clock. Up, showered and dressed.

In black. Only the flame of her hair provided vivid colour in the harsh landscape. And she was in the process of coiling it into a tight bun when she followed him out to the dining room, where he'd set her breakfast tray.

Ari resisted the urge to pull her hands away from her task. He also resisted the urge to command her to change her clothes.

She finished securing her hair and turned to him. Her gaze met his for a moment before travelling over his body.

Noting his attire, she looked back up. 'Have you slept at all?'

'No,' he replied, vaguely disturbed by his anger at her choice of clothes.

A look of concern crossed her eyes. He allowed it to touch him for a second, two seconds, before he looked away.

'Sit down. Drink your tea and have some of those dry crackers. They'll calm any nausea that triggers morning sickness.'

She looked at the tray and wrinkled her nose. 'Too late. I've already thrown up twice.'

He forced away the anxiety that tightened his nape. 'Drink it anyway.'

She sat and he poured her tea and passed it to her, noting the anxious glances she sent his way. Part of him wanted to reassure her. He curbed the feeling because he knew the road ahead wouldn't be easy.

'Aren't you having anything?'

'No. Until we find out which smells trigger your nausea, I'll eat my meals separately.'

'How come you know so much about morning sickness and nausea triggers?'

Ice formed in his belly, stealing his breath. But it was nothing compared to the pain that ripped through his heart as the guilt and fear returned twice as forcefully.

He looked up and saw the anxiety stamped on her face.

'Ari?'

'I know because my wife was four months pregnant with our first child when she died.'

Her cup clattered onto the saucer and her features paled. 'Oh, my God. I'm… I don't know what to say. I'm sorry for—'

He slashed a hand through the air, unwilling to dwell on the past, unwilling to let her see the devastation that still had the power to shred his insides.

They had more important things to discuss than the subject of his hubris.

'Drink your tea, Perla. We have a lot to discuss.'

The shock of his revelation still clear in her eyes, she slowly picked up her cup and took another tiny sip. He waited until she'd eaten a cracker before he spoke.

'Do you have any health issues that I should know about?'

She placed her cup down. 'I'm allergic to shellfish but, aside from that, I've always been healthy and Morgan's health insurance provided me with annual check-ups. They always came back clean.'

The mention of her husband's name made his fists clench but he forced the feeling away. He needed to get over the fact that she'd been another man's wife only a short time ago.

'Good. Then we'll postpone a thorough health check until we return to London.'

Her eyes connected with his. 'We're returning to London?'

'Yes.'

'Why?'

'Because London is where we will be married.'

CHAPTER TEN

'No.'

'You've already said that. Twice.'

'I believe in making things crystal-clear so there's no misunderstanding. I won't marry you.'

Perla watched his nostrils pinch in that way that told her he was hanging onto his control by a thread. But the emotions coursing through her eroded any concern for his control or lack thereof.

Who would've believed that a proposal of marriage could bring so much pain? But devastating pain was exactly what ravaged her as they faced each other across his wide living room like two boxers about to engage in a fight.

'You've yet to give me a reason why not.'

'And you've yet to give me a valid reason why I should. Presumably it's because I'm pregnant. Regardless, the answer is still no.'

'Perla—'

'No is no, Ari.' Her hands shook as she thought back to what she'd been through the last three years. 'I got married under false pretences three years ago. I won't do it again, no matter the reason.'

His eyes sparked with curiosity. 'Explain.'

She paused. Could she reveal the final humiliation? 'I've already told you my marriage was… difficult. I also know how you feel about me and the circumstances under which we met. No matter how much you try to deny it, I know you despise what happened between us. Trust me, losing my virginity to a man who's mourning his dead wife on the anniversary of her death is bad enough. I refuse to become trapped in another sham of a marriage where I'm second best.'

She ground to a halt at his white-faced shock.

'Your *virginity?*' he rasped in a tone that could've flayed stone.

Perla flinched. Of course. Of all the things she'd said, that was the one he'd have picked up on. Turning around, she squeezed her eyes shut as the familiar shame dredged through her stomach.

'Perla.' He was right behind her, standing so close his breath washed over her exposed nape, making a shiver course through her. 'Did you just say you were a virgin when we slept together?' he asked, his voice spiked with emotions she couldn't name.

Clenching her hands into tight fists, she struggled to breathe. 'Yes.'

'Turn around.'

'No.'

'You really need to stop defying me so much. There are some things I will let slide. This isn't one of them. Turn around,' he demanded, more forcefully this time.

Heart in her throat, she opened her eyes and turned. The gold flecks in his eyes stood out with the intensity of his stare. 'You were married for three years. How were you still a virgin on your husband's death?'

She affected a shrug that felt far from casual. 'We never got round to it, I guess.'

He gripped her shoulders in an implacable hold. 'This is not the time to be facetious. Tell me how Lowell could have a woman such as you in his bed and walk away. Why a woman who could drive any red-blooded man to his knees with just one look could remain a virgin for so long within the bounds of marriage.'

'Because I did nothing for him!'

He frowned. 'You refused to sleep with him?'

She laughed, or rather she attempted to laugh. The sound scraped her throat and emerged a ragged croak. 'On the contrary, I threw myself at him. Hell, I even tried to seduce him *before* and after we were married. He suggested we wait. Stupid me, I thought it was the height of *romantic*; that he was being *noble!* But it turned out he didn't want me. You want to know why? Because my husband told me on our wedding night that he was gay!'

Hazel eyes widened. 'Lowell was gay?'

'I'm surprised you don't know, considering where he was when your investigators found him in Thailand.'

'We knew he'd taken residence in a disreputable part of Bangkok when he was found but I assumed...'

'He was whoring it up with women? No, Ari, the man I married was probably shacked up with a boyfriend when your men caught up with him. I didn't need to be a genius to read between the lines. And I don't need a crystal ball to know he changed the terms of his contract and plotted to crash the Pantelides tanker because he needed money to fund his secret life and the drug habit that killed him.' Raw humiliation threatened to consume her whole, especially when he let out a crude curse.

'Perla *mou*...'

'No, I don't want to talk about this any more. And I don't want to discuss marriage. You're proposing because I'm pregnant but nothing will ever convince me to get married again.'

'Not even the welfare of your child?'

She paled and he let out another curse. Swinging her into his arms, he walked to the sofa and sat down with her in his lap.

'This child means everything to me. I intend to give it everything it needs,' she whispered fiercely.

'Except a stable home and the unity of both parents.'

'That's a low blow, Ari. You had that for a while. But it didn't turn out great for you either, did it?' She regretted her answer but she had to fight back. She was no longer fighting for just herself. She had her baby to think of.

Ari's arms tightened around her. 'Our marriage will be different.'

'You cannot possibly know that.'

'I'm determined to win this fight, Perla.'

'Why does it have to be a fight?'

'Because you're resisting my every effort to make you see sense.'

'Just because I don't see things your way doesn't mean it's nonsense. If this hadn't happened, would *you* have ever remarried?'

The tightening of his jaw and the way his eyelids swept down gave her the answer she needed. 'So why does it have to be different for me?'

'Because this is no longer just about you.'

Simple words that made her breath catch. 'I know. But this is emotional blackmail.' And she refused to succumb to blackmail of any sort ever again.

'It's the truth. Tell me what your plan is for our child. Do you intend to return to your former in-laws after he or she is born, live with Lowell's parents with another man's child?'

A shiver went through her. 'Of course not. I'll find another place to live.'

'And when the child is older? What then?'

'I'll find adequate childcare and continue my career. Millions of women do it every day. Why should I be any different?'

'Because this child is not just any child. It is a Pantelides. Whether you want to admit it or not, that makes it different from any other child.'

'I know you like to think you're special but—'

'No buts, Perla. I've lost one unborn child.' His gaze dropped to her flat stomach and he swallowed hard. 'If I'm lucky enough to become a father for a second time, nothing and no one will keep me from my child.'

A stalemate.

Despite knowing it was temporary, she hung onto the stalemate as Ari's private jet raced them towards Bermuda and the Pantelides resort project she'd undertaken what seemed like a thousand years ago.

It was hard to fathom that it'd been barely eighteen hours since she'd discovered she was carrying Ari's child.

Even harder to believe she'd agreed to give him an answer in the time the marriage licence would take to be ready.

But the look on his face when he'd made his vow had shaken her to the core. Shaken her into considering the fact that he meant it when he said he wanted a full-time role in their child's life.

After what she had been through, shoved from foster home to foster home and then eventually spat out at eighteen, did she not owe it to her child to give it the best care possible?

But then could she bear to tie herself to another man who clearly did not want her for herself? Morgan had used her to hide his true sexual orientation from those he believed would judge him.

With Ari, it was simply the fact that she carried his heir.

A wave of sadness washed over her and the tablet she was supposed to be using to jot down ideas for the resort opening blurred as tears welled in her eyes.

Tears. Another symptom of her pregnancy she couldn't seem to stem. She brushed them away and looked up to find Ari watching her.

'What's wrong?'

'I seem to have discovered the pregnancy hormone that lets me cry at the drop of a hat. I should hire myself out to Hollywood.'

He stood from his wide leather seat and approached her with one hand outstretched. 'Come with me,' he commanded.

'Where are we going?' she asked, although she found herself putting her hand in his, allowing him to draw her up.

'We don't land for an hour and a half. You should take the time to rest.'

She stopped. 'I'm pregnant, not sick. I don't need to rest.'

'But you will. Or I'll turn this plane around and we can head to London.'

'I have work to do, Ari—'

'You were staring at a blank screen on your tablet.'

'I was *strategising.*'

'Yes, and it was so effective you were in tears.' He placed a firm hand on her waist and propelled her forward. He opened the cabin door and she entered a large, sumptuously appointed bedroom. The gold-and-blue décor screamed opulent sophistication but it was the bed that drew her attention. King-sized and high, it was piled with pillows and covered with a gold silk spread that begged to be touched.

Moving forward, she did just that, then went one better and sat on the edge of the bed. The firm mattress gave a little beneath her and, on a whim, she kicked off her shoes and scooted backwards just as a large yawn caught her unawares.

She looked up to find Ari regarding her with an amused expression. 'Fine. I can probably do with a little rest.'

He moved forward and started removing the cufflinks from his shirt. As he folded the sleeves back, he toed off his shoes.

'What are you doing?'

'What does it look like?'

'But…' She stopped as she recalled that he'd been up all night. It suddenly struck her that he'd taken care of her all through the shocking discovery of her pregnancy and afterwards while he'd neglected his own needs.

She could insist he return to the cabin but that would be unnecessarily mean and, really, there was more than enough room on the bed for both of them. It wasn't as if he was about to tear her clothes off and make mad, passionate love to her.

They'd moved past that.

She pushed away the ache that lodged in her heart at the thought and lifted the cover.

The smile he gave her didn't quite reach his eyes and she noticed the tension lines around his mouth when he got into bed.

Expecting him to relax against the pillow, she held her breath when he turned sideways and propped his head on his curved arm. Hypnotic eyes travelled over her hair. 'You'll be much more comfortable if you take your hair down.'

'I don't think so. My hair has got me into too much trouble around you and your inner ten-year-old. It's staying up.'

Her hair had been an explosive subject between them. Far be it from her to tempt fate. Or, worse still, for her to tempt fate only to find fate couldn't care less.

His mouth twisted. 'Please yourself.' He relaxed against the pillows, crossed his hands over his chest and closed his eyes. Within minutes, his even breathing echoed softly through the room.

She stared because she couldn't help herself. And because, like the first time she'd watched him sleep, Ari's transformation in repose was breathtaking.

But now she knew the reason behind the constant torment that lurked in his eyes and the bone-deep weariness etched into his face, she was thankful he received peace in sleep.

For the first time since he'd told her, she let herself think of just what Ari had lost. Losing his wife was devastating enough, but his unborn child, too? Was it any wonder he'd been so desolate that day at Macdonald Hall?

Was it any wonder he'd wanted to find oblivion? Her heart ached and tears clouded her eyes all over again.

God, this needed to stop or she'd be a basket case long before this child was born. She couldn't afford to be a basket case. Couldn't afford anything other than her complete wits about her, her mind *and* her heart intact. She'd been through too much to put her emotions on the line again. Until she could find a way to guarantee that, there was no way she could consider Ari's proposal.

Because there were times when he showed her

kindness that her foolish heart believed he could care for her.

And that was a slippery slope to heartache she had no intention of skidding down…

She woke to the sound of a steady heartbeat beneath her ear and a warm, familiar scent in her nostrils. But it was the fingers splayed over her stomach that made her eyes slowly drift open.

Ari was awake, his gaze fixed on her flat belly. She must have curled closer to his side of the bed in her sleep because he had one arm clamped around her while his other rested on her stomach.

As she watched him, a wave of despair washed over his face. The emotion was so strong her breath caught. He heard it and his eyes flew to hers. He started to withdraw, but she held his hand in place.

'What happened to her?' she asked softly.

He froze and his features shuttered. For several minutes she thought he wouldn't answer. 'She had a weak heart. The doctors were divided on whether she could carry a child to term without it causing a severe strain on her heart. I warned her it was too risky. She chose to side with the more optimistic doctors. Her heart gave out in her second trimester.'

The naked devastation in his voice slashed her insides. 'And you blame yourself.'

That was why the news of her pregnancy didn't

bring joy. The look on his face had been one of deep, wretched torment.

His smile was grim as his eyes were bleak. 'Despite my fears, I let myself be convinced she would be all right. That our child would be all right. They both died.'

'Ari, you can't—'

He pulled away and got out of bed. 'We are not having this conversation now, Perla. It's time to leave the plane. We landed ten minutes ago.'

The Pantelides Bermuda was another architectural work of art. The blueprints and plans Ari had shown her at the restaurant were nowhere near as awe-inspiring as the real thing.

The long, palm-tree-lined drive along a private road gave way to six sprawling buildings linked together by curved wooden bridges.

Multi-roomed suites, each one containing a wide wooden deck, an infinity pool and a luxurious spa, faced a stunning private white-sanded beach. Four-poster beds built with local carved wood soared up to vaulted ceilings and crown mouldings that lent an air of old-world elegance, blending old and new in exquisite symmetry.

The exclusive three-storey casino made entirely of triple-paned glass was set away from the main resort on giant transparent stilts and accessed by private boats manned by discreet security guards.

From the resort, the building seemed to be floating on water.

Once their luggage was loaded into an air-conditioned SUV, Ari turned to her. 'We'll take the full tour later. Right now I'll introduce you to your chef.'

'As long as it's not to another bed and a command to "rest", we're okay.'

His lips twisted but he said nothing as he climbed in beside her and drove them to their villa at the southernmost point of the resort.

The sight of the turquoise waters gave her another idea for the opening. 'I think I'll add scuba-diving to the activities.'

'Great. Consider rowing too.'

'Rowing?'

'Sakis and Brianna are joining us for a couple of days before the guests arrive. Sometimes the waters around here get a little choppy but I intend to row with Sakis. I'll let you know how I rate it.'

'That would be great, thanks.'

There was no sign of the ragged pain she'd seen on his face on the plane. He was back to Arion Pantelides, luxury hotel mogul and master of all he surveyed.

She held her breath when they reached the villa and the staff asked where to place their luggage.

'I'll take the smaller suite. You take the master suite,' Ari said.

Perla wasn't sure why her stomach fell with disappointment. Had she really thought he would insist on joint sleeping arrangements? Nothing had changed since yesterday aside from the fact that their indiscretions had resulted in a child. Sexually, they were done with each other.

Still she couldn't suppress her rising desolation as he walked away. With two personal butlers seeing to the unpacking, Perla changed into the only bikini she owned and walked from room to room, acquainting herself with the layout of the villa. It was as she entered the solarium that she noticed the repeating item in each room.

She turned as Ari walked in. 'You've had an epi pen placed in each room?' she asked, her heart flipping over when she noticed he'd changed into khaki shorts and a white T-shirt.

'Yes,' he answered simply.

The thoughtfulness behind the gesture was so alien, she blurted, 'Why?'

He paused on the way to the French windows that led to the teak-floored deck, changed course and came to stand in front of her. This close, his proximity wreaked havoc with her pulse rate. Reaching out, he brushed his fingers down her cheek.

'I'm not taking any chances this time, Perla. Not with you, not with this baby.' His voice was a solid, solemn vow that struck deep into her heart.

Her eyes prickled and she sniffed hard. 'Are you determined to make me cry again?'

He grimaced and dropped his hand. 'Perhaps I need to learn to accept that tears are par for the course. Come and meet Peter, your chef.'

Slowly she followed him outside into the sunshine, desperately trying to get her wayward emotions under control. 'I really don't need a personal chef.'

'It is already done, *glikia mou*, so you have to live with it.'

She was trying to decipher the Greek endearment when a man dressed in chef whites stepped forward from behind the table where he'd been slicing fresh fruit.

'Your fruit platter is coming right up. And for lunch I have some freshly grilled chicken kebabs with a green salad. If you need anything else, let me know.'

Ari steered her towards twin loungers by the pool. As they sat down, his phone pinged. The huge smile that split his face as he read the text made her breath catch.

'Theo is coming down too. He'll be here at the end of the week.'

A pang of envy spilled into her heart. 'You're very close, aren't you?'

He looked up and shrugged. 'They're my family. They mean everything to me.'

The simple statement made more tears prickle her eyes. He saw it and frowned. 'Perla?'

'You're so lucky. I mean...you've had tragedy,

of course, but you've remained close with your family and that's…that's…'

He watched her with keen eyes. 'It's something you've never had.'

'No.'

He set his phone aside. 'Marry me and you can have it too.'

Her heart lurched and temptation shot hope into her heart. But still her instincts shrieked dire warning.

'It's not that simple. I can't…'

His face hardened. 'For the sake of this child we have to make sacrifices, Perla.'

'What do you mean?'

'I mean we both agree we're not an ideal match but we need to look beyond that to what's best for our child. Whatever lofty ideas you have of being an ideal single parent will always pale in comparison to what we can provide as a united family. That is the bottom line.'

'That may be your bottom line. It's not mine. I think it's more important that this child grows up in a loving environment.'

His face hardened further. 'And you don't think we can provide that?'

She held her breath until Peter had delivered the fruit platters and returned to the far side of the deck where he was preparing their lunch. 'Come on, Ari. After what you've been through, what we've both been through—'

'My past has nothing to do with this.'

Her heart sank. 'If you believe that then I'm going to need even more time to consider your proposal.'

'What the hell are you saying, Perla?'

'I'm saying you've been hurt and devastated. We've both been. We need to factor that into how much that will impact our child's welfare.'

'So you want me to spill my feelings to you before you consider marrying me.'

'No. But we need to get past the bitterness and deal with the pain before we can move on. That aside, we've barely spent more than forty-eight hours in each other's company.'

His eyes gleamed. 'And a good portion of that time we spent having sex. At least we know we're compatible in the bedroom.'

Heat crawled over her skin and burrowed inside to sting parts of her body she didn't want to think about right now. 'How does that help in bringing up a child?'

His gaze drifted over her flushed skin, and his smile held a great deal of mockery. 'You'd be surprised how compliant a well-sated man can be.'

She speared a piece of papaya with her fork as her face flamed. 'Well, I wouldn't know. I didn't succeed in that department during my marriage.'

He stiffened. 'You were wasting your passion on the wrong man. Our marriage will be different.'

'So…so you intend for us to…'

'Have sex? Yes, Perla. I have no intention of living like a monk.'

So she had an answer as to how the physical part of their marriage would be. But no clue as to the emotional. Could she contemplate a future with him, knowing he would never be emotionally available?

No. Sex, as she'd discovered, was great. But it would never be enough in the long run.

Despite losing her appetite, she forced herself to eat a few more chunks of fruit and summoned a smile when the staff cleared away their plates.

She looked up to find Ari staring at her, the question clear in his eyes. 'We agreed to a week, Ari.'

His lips compressed. 'What will be different in a week's time that we can't resolve today?'

Her hands shook and she took a sip of water. 'Maybe I can convince you to talk to me a little bit more.'

His eyes narrowed. 'And will this therapy session be a two-way thing?'

She'd already told him the most humiliating secret, but the deeper secret, the yearning for a connection, to belong… It was that deep yearning that had swayed her into Morgan's path in the first place. Could she share that with Ari?

She took a deep breath. 'I'm willing to try if you are. But we both have to be committed to try.'

'Perla…' His voice held mild disgruntlement.

'We agreed on a week. All I'm doing is adding a tiny addendum. You owe our child, at the very least.'

Ari felt his insides tighten and fought the need to demand an answer right there and then. With each minute that ticked past, he felt more and more on edge, as if some unforeseen wrecking ball hovered just beyond the horizon, ready to smash through the quiet joy bubbling beneath his skin.

Perla was right. He'd never intended to marry again, but waking up next to Perla on the plane to find her curled up so trustingly against him, he'd begun to dare to believe that he could have another chance to reclaim what he'd lost.

A part of him had died with Sofia and their unborn child. But he could forge a new family, be the father he'd always wanted to be, the one his own father had failed so comprehensively to be.

But in this he knew he had to be patient, no matter how much it killed him.

'I'm not a patient man.'

His chest tightened as her mouth curved in a tiny relieved smile. 'I'm learning that. Maybe I should also confess I'm a stubborn woman.'

His gaze flew to her hair and his groin tightened. He wryly admitted that his need to speed things up also stemmed from the fact that as a married man he wouldn't have to hold back on the need that clawed relentlessly through him day and night.

'Fine. I agree that we use this week to learn some more about each other.'

She smiled at Peter as he delivered their main course. Then her eyes returned to Ari. 'Does that mean I can ask you whatever I want?'

He'd opened that particular door. Attempting to slam it shut now would only make things worse. He gave a single curt nod and saw the speculative smile that curved her full mouth.

'Word of warning, though. I give as good as I get. And I don't always play fair.'

Her smile disappeared and Ari couldn't stop the laugh that rumbled out at her startled look.

He tore into his lunch and watched with satisfaction as she consumed hers. They were polishing off the last of the salad when she glanced furtively at him.

'Do your brothers know that I'm…pregnant?'

'No, I haven't told them yet. Ideally, I'd like to announce the pregnancy and our intended marriage at the same time.'

Her gaze slid from his and he forced himself not to react. 'Um…okay.'

Feeling the restlessness that had taken up residence in his body clamouring through him again, he got up. 'Time for the full tour, then I'll let you get to work.'

CHAPTER ELEVEN

THE DAYS PASSED in a blur of activity and by the time Sakis and Brianna arrived on Thursday afternoon, Perla had everything in place in anticipation for when the VIP guests arrived on Sunday.

Unlike their first meeting, Sakis Pantelides's smile was openly friendly if a lot speculative. She read the same keen interest in Brianna's stunning blue eyes.

'Ari tells me you're putting on a spectacular list of events for the opening.'

'He should know. He's been slave-driving me up the wall with his endless demands for perfection. Perhaps now you're here, you can get him out of my hair for an hour or two.'

Brianna laughed as she hugged her husband's arm. 'That seems to be a common trait amongst the Pantelides men. They never know when to leave well enough alone and trust us women to get on with it.'

Her husband sent her an indulgent smile so full

of adoration Perla's heart snagged in her chest then dropped to her stomach in envy.

'Asking me to leave you alone is like asking the lark to stop singing first thing in the morning. It's simply impossible, *agapita*.'

A blush raced up her face and the powerful passion that arced between them made Perla look away.

Sakis turned to her. 'Where is my brother, anyway?'

'He's getting the scull ready for your rowing session this afternoon. I believe he wants to hit the water the moment Theo arrives,' she said.

What she didn't add was that Ari had been growing steadily more restless as the days had progressed this week. This morning they'd snapped at each other over breakfast, after which he'd disappeared with a curt instruction for her to take things easy. Or else...

God, why had she deluded herself into thinking they'd learn *nice* things about each other this week? So far she'd learned that even though he'd stated that he was happy for her to carry on working, he intended to keep a close eye on her at all times.

She only had to think of a need for it to materialise. Meals and snacks appeared minutes before cravings hit and there was always someone with a golf buggy, a wide-brimmed hat or a cool drink nearby.

That he also fully intended to extract a *yes* from her as soon as he could was also clear. As for the heated looks he'd sent her whenever she walked into his presence…

She shook her head and focused to find two pairs of eyes trained on her. 'Um…the concierge's assistant will escort you to your villa and I'll let Ari know you're here.'

With a smile she knew was a little strained, she walked away. After triple-checking everything on her list and clucking with impatience because she knew she was dawdling, she jumped into her allotted SUV and drove down to their villa.

Ari was in the middle of a phone call when she walked into the cool, brightly lit living room. He advanced until he stood in front of her but carried on his conversation, one hand idly playing with her loose hair.

She'd started their stay by wearing it up but Ari had found every opportunity to free it until she'd given up. There were some fights that just weren't worth the effort.

She didn't follow his conversation because it was conducted in rapid-fire Greek. But even if he'd spoken English, she wouldn't have followed it because of the feverish emotions coursing through her at his touch.

Each day since they arrived at the resort he'd laid assault to her senses like this, touching her whenever she was within a few feet, grazing his fingers over her stomach in a possessive move that sent her emotions into free fall every time. That had been when he wasn't snapping at her.

To say their time together so far had been a roller coaster would be an understatement.

She heard him end the call as his thumb traced over her mouth. Slowly he lowered the phone and his head began to descend.

'Were you looking for me?' he murmured.

'Yes. Your brother and Brianna are here.'

'I know. Sakis called me ten minutes ago.' His head moved closer. 'Theo is also on his way from the airport. He'll be here in less than ten minutes. He wants to row straight away so I've had the equipment sent down to the water.'

His lips flitted over hers and she tried to pull back. 'Ari…don't.'

He stiffened slightly. 'I've been a bear towards you all week. Let me apologise,' he coaxed in that deep, hypnotic voice.

Her breath gushed out of her as he sealed her lips with his. Their mingled groan echoed around the room, then faded away to be replaced with harsh breathing. They strained towards each other until she could feel the solid imprint of his body and the even more rigid outline of his arousal against her belly.

The need that tore through her made her spear her hands through his hair. With a deep groan he picked her up and carried her to the sofa without breaking their kiss.

He was kissing his way down her neck when she finally came to her senses.

'No. Stop!'

He raised his head slowly, his eyes sizzling pools of need and frustration. 'Why the hell should I?' he growled.

'We can't...you can't use sex to apologise. Saying you're sorry is enough.'

A mirthless smile tilted one corner of his mouth. 'You really are naïve, aren't you?'

She blushed fiercely. 'Perhaps, but I also know that sex can confuse issues. You've been grumpy for days because you weren't getting your way. Sex will not achieve what you want.'

His eyes gleamed as he reared back. 'But it will make me feel a whole lot better. And you can deny it all you want but it will make you feel better too.'

She couldn't deny it but neither was she going to admit it. She sat up and straightened her clothes. The black sundress wasn't exactly appropriate for the tropics but it seemed black was all she'd packed. 'Anyway, we can't. We have guests who require our attention. But don't think I haven't noticed that every time I try to get you to talk to me like we agreed, you find something else for me to do!'

He stiffened and jerked to his feet. 'You're asking a man who has kept his innermost thoughts hidden most of his life to bare his soul, *glikia mou*. It's not as simple as hitting play on a machine,' he said, his voice charged with the echo of painful memory.

Her heart twisted for him, but she pressed on. Deep inside, she'd begun to hope that this would be the way to reach him, the way they could both move forward and begin the tentative steps to building a solid platform for their child. 'I know that. Of course I know that. But, as difficult as it is, we have to give it a shot, Ari.'

Slowly, he inhaled. Then he nodded and held out his hand to her. 'We will. Before we leave here. Now, you can come and watch me row my sexual frustration away. That will be your entertainment for the afternoon.'

She let herself be pulled up and felt some of her trepidation melt away. Immediately, thoughts that had hovered on the edge of her mind crowded in. Thoughts that involved whether she and Ari could make a marriage work despite all their baggage. That he seemed to believe it was possible had slowly eroded her own scepticism as the week had crept on.

The way Ari had taken care of her since her pregnancy came to light, she didn't doubt now that he would provide a parent's utter devotion and stability. And perhaps, over time, that devotion would spill onto her.

Her heart lurched painfully.

Morgan had shaken the foundation of her beliefs. But she'd discovered in the last few weeks that he hadn't totally annihilated her self-confidence. It was that renewed self-confidence that made her want even better for herself and her child.

At least, with Ari, she knew the lay of the land going in. The events of his past might mean he never cared deeply for her. So the only thing that she needed to be sure of was whether she could live without the love she'd been so desperate for the first time round.

Before we leave here...

She pushed away the lingering trepidation and concentrated on getting in the electric buggy that would take them down to the water, although it was hard not to keep glancing at Ari's bare thighs as he drove.

The youngest Pantelides was already on the waterfront with Sakis when they arrived.

Theo Pantelides was as tall as Ari but broader-shouldered with the same jet-black hair, although his bore no hint of the grey sprinkled at Ari's temples.

Equally as gorgeous, his eyes were several shades lighter than Ari's hazel and held the same speculation as Sakis's when they rested on her.

'So I finally meet the woman who's caused quite the stir at Pantelides HQ.'

'Theo...' Ari growled a mild warning.

Theo's smile was unrepentant as he held out a closed fist to her. A smile twitching at her lips, she touched her knuckles to his in a bemused fist bump.

'About time someone shook him out of his doldrums,' he added with a wink.

Sakis laughed and Brianna grinned but Ari's narrow-eyed stare held no mirth.

'Tell me you're ready to get your ass whipped and I'll happily oblige you,' he said through clenched teeth.

'Any time, old man.'

Ari's jaw clenched harder but the hand he clamped on his brother's shoulder to push him towards the boat was so affectionate it brought a lump to Perla's throat. He disappeared into the specially built boathouse and emerged minutes later dressed in a dark gold rowing suit that moulded to his body.

Perla tried not to stare at the perfect specimen of man that was Arion Pantelides but when he grabbed the end of the scull and hefted it over his shoulders, she struggled to get air past her restricted throat into her lungs.

Purely for self-preservation, she looked away. Then immediately looked back.

'God, don't even try to resist that. Don't get me wrong, I think Sakis is the best-looking of the bunch, but the three of them together like this, even I find it hard to breathe, never mind keep my eyes solely on my husband,' Brianna muttered.

She grinned at Perla's shocked laugh, fanned herself and moved closer to the edge of the viewing bench to watch the men set their scull on the water and climb in.

Sakis took the front seat, Theo the middle and Ari the last. They sank their oars into the water. Theo rolled his shoulders and laughed when Ari admonished him to be still.

Their chests rose and fell in rhythm, once, twice. Then they struck away from shore in flawless synchronicity.

'Wow.'

'I know, right? I've watched them row many times but I never get over how perfect they look together.'

Again Perla felt that tiny pang of jealousy. But she couldn't help but wonder if this could be her baby's life if she agreed to what Ari wanted. Her child, and by definition she, could be a part of this…togetherness. She didn't have to be on the outside looking in like she had her whole life. She could give her baby a ready-made family who would cherish him or her.

She watched the men row, her eyes continually drawn to Ari, who now had a grin on his face despite the determination in his eyes.

'Ari seems different.'

Perla jumped and turned to Brianna to find those incisive blue eyes on her. 'Um…is he?'

Brianna nodded. 'At the funeral he seemed ready to smash everyone's head in. Today he looks as if the only person whose head is in danger is Theo, which, considering that's par for the course, is worth mentioning.'

'And you think I have something to do with that?'

'Definitely. You and…that, I'm guessing.'

She followed Brianna's gaze to where her hand rested on her stomach. With a gasp, Perla snatched her hand away but not before Brianna gave her a sympathetic smile.

'I…no one knows,' she said hurriedly.

'Don't worry, your secret's safe with me.' Her hand rose to rest over her own stomach. 'I have a secret of my own. Although I have a feeling it won't remain a secret for long. Sakis has been bursting to tell the whole world. But I'm guessing he'll start with his brothers for now.'

'Congratulations,' Perla offered. Then curiosity made her blurt, 'How do you feel?'

'Frankly? Scared out of my mind. I didn't have the best of childhoods so I don't have a role model to fall back on. Sakis tells me I'll be a great mother but I think he's hopelessly biased.' Her smile was tinged with anxiety but full of love as her gaze swung back to the men. 'What about you?'

'Honestly, between Ari's determination to get

me to marry him and the job I have to do here, I haven't had time to be scared, but—'

'Ari asked you to marry him?' Brianna's eyes were wide with surprise. 'That's huge! I presume he's told you what happened to his wife?'

Perla nodded.

'He wouldn't have made the decision easily.'

'He only wants to marry because of his child.'

Brianna frowned. 'I don't think so. I don't want to scare you but the reality is that every one in four pregnancies ends in miscarriage. If all he wanted was to give the baby respectability, he'd have waited until it was born to ask you to marry him.'

Perla shook her head, refusing to even begin to hope. 'Besides the baby, there's really nothing like that between us.'

'But there is *something*. There's incredible chemistry. Don't knock the power of great sex.'

She gasped. 'That's what he said,' she said then blushed as she realised what she'd let slip.

Brianna laughed. 'I knew there was an alpha horn dog beneath all that suave Pantelides exterior. Now let's go and cheer our boys home before I give in to the urge to ask for details I have no business knowing.'

She jumped up and headed towards the waterfront. Perla followed at a slower pace and got there in time to see the brothers embrace at the news of Brianna's pregnancy.

Ari's gaze drifted to her as Sakis pulled his wife close and kissed her. His gaze dropped to her stomach but he said nothing, only helped his brothers stow the scull and oars in the boathouse before they all piled into the buggies to head back to their villas.

Dinner that evening turned into a family celebration, one that hammered home to Perla just what she could be missing out on if she refused Ari's proposal. All through the evening his eyes kept straying to her, the intent in their depths clear and determined.

By the time she excused herself and returned to her suite, her mind was in turmoil.

That turmoil continued for the next three days. Thankfully, she had no time to think.

From the moment the first luxury SUV rolled in with the guests her days turned manic. She barely saw Ari because he was equally busy entertaining guests in the plushly equipped casino while she dealt with organising the guests and directing the activities she'd planned for them.

She was busy sorting out the sky-diving group and pairing them with their instructors and guests on the last day when she heard a familiar voice.

She looked up to see Selena Hamilton heading towards her.

Perla's mouth dropped open before she could stop herself.

'So, what do you think?' Selena trilled, patting her new russet-coloured curls.

Perla forced a smile. 'You look great.'

Selena's smile slipped a fraction. 'I'm glad you think so. Roger thinks I look awful. What does he know, right?' She forced a laugh that didn't touch her curiously over-bright eyes.

Roger Hamilton strolled in at that moment. He completely ignored his wife and, grabbing Perla, kissed her on both cheeks.

'Sign me up for whatever you're organising, darling! I'm all yours.'

Behind him, Ari entered the room and froze to a halt. The thunderous look in his eyes made her stomach flip but she managed to keep the smile on her face as he walked to where she stood. Seeing the look he directed at Roger, she glared at him and shook her head once. His jaw clenched but he exchanged pleasantries until the instructor called for them to suit up.

Ari's hand slid over her nape and tilted her head up to meet his descending kiss. It was hard and quick. 'You take care of Hamilton, *glikia mou*. Or I will,' he muttered. Then he was gone.

Breathing a sigh of relief, she turned around just as Selena returned to her side. Before she could utter a word, Selena grabbed her arm. 'I think Roger is going to leave me,' she whispered fiercely.

'Are you sure?'

Her frenzied nodding made her curls bounce wildly. 'I think he's having an affair.' Her scarlet-painted lips wobbled and her eyes widened.

'You could be wrong…'

'What if I'm not? I can't live without him. He's everything I've ever wanted but I can see him slipping away from me.' Tears filled her green eyes.

'Selena, I don't think you should go sky-diving if you're feeling like that.'

She swiped her tears with perfectly manicured fingers. 'Nonsense. Roger wants to go sky-diving so I'm going with him.'

But a glance at Roger, who was busy flirting with a female instructor, suggested he had no interest in what his wife wanted. Perla glanced at Selena again and worry gnawed at her. Selena's glazed eyes suggested she was under the influence of something other than unhappiness. But there was no diplomatic way to ask without causing offence.

Gnawing at her bottom lip, she followed the guests out to the air-conditioned buses that would take them to the airstrip. Then climbed in with them.

'Where the hell is she?' Ari demanded for the fifth time. The concierge manager paled and reached for his phone again.

'I'm sorry, sir, but we think she may have joined one of the guest events.'

'You *think*? Try her phone again.'

The manager hurried to do his bidding. When he shook his head regretfully, Ari curbed the need to punch a hole in the desk.

'Giving your staff hell?' came a droll voice from behind him.

'Not now, Sakis.'

'Why? What's wrong?'

'I'm trying to find Perla. No one's seen her in the last hour.'

'And this is worrying because…?'

Ari pursed his lips. 'She's supposed to be at the villa, having lunch.'

He looked up as the assistant manager hurried forward. 'Mr Pantelides, I've just been told by one of the drivers that Mrs Lowell joined the sky-diving guests.'

For a moment, he couldn't compute the information. 'She *what?*'

The voices that responded were drowned out by the blood thundering in his ears. When his arm was grabbed in a firm hold and he was propelled down a hallway, he did not protest.

He heard a door shut behind him seconds before Sakis pushed him into a seat.

'Talk to me, Ari. What the hell is going on?'

He speared both hands into his hair and tried to stem the terror rushing through him. 'It's probably nothing. She can't possibly have gone *sky-diving…*'

'Yeah…that's what your man said.'

He tried to swallow. 'Well…she can't have.'

'Why not? If she's qualified—'

'Sakis. She's pregnant.'

His brother's mouth dropped open seconds before the colour leached from his face. They both leapt for the phone on his desk but Ari was quicker. 'I need your fastest driver out front in the next ten seconds.'

Sakis wrenched the door open. They passed Theo in the hallway and one dark look from Ari and his brother stemmed whatever wisecrack he'd been about to utter.

In silence, he fell into step beside them.

The journey to the airstrip was the longest of Ari's life.

Horrific scenarios he couldn't stem tumbled through his mind and the fingers that continually clawed through his hair shook uncontrollably.

Brightly coloured parachutes slowly loomed into view as their SUV roared down towards the designated area on the edge of the parachute landing site.

Theos, surely she hadn't…

Ari was out of the car before it'd come to a screeching halt. He heard the thunder of running feet behind him as his brothers followed him.

One by one he watched the eight parachutes drop lower, his heart hammering as he rushed from one to the other.

None of them were Perla.

'Ari?' He whirled round to find her stepping down from the air-conditioned bus, Selena Hamilton following behind her. Relief was followed closely by volcanic anger. This time, there were no feet thundering behind him as he sprinted to the bus.

He skidded to a halt in front of her. She started to speak. '*Not. One. Word.*'

Her mouth dropped open. Without giving her a chance to respond, he swung her up in his arms and marched her to the SUV parked a hundred yards away.

'Out,' he growled. The driver jumped out and held out the keys. He placed her in the passenger seat, secured her seat belt and ignored his brothers as he got in and slammed the door.

'I'm guessing we have to find our own ride back?' Theo quipped to Sakis.

Ari turned the ignition and peeled out of the airstrip, his heartbeat a deafening roar in his ears.

The journey to the villa took less than ten minutes. This time he didn't help her out. He headed straight into the villa and sought out the butler.

'I want you and your staff to take a break. Don't return until I tell you to.'

He returned to the living room to see the staff hurrying out and Perla standing in the hallway, her face pale and her teeth worrying her lower lip.

'Ari, please. You're scaring me.'

He threw the car keys across the room and watched them hit the wall and bounce on the marble floor.

'*I'm* scaring *you?*'

Her arched brows spiked upward. 'Can we try less snarling and more coherence?'

'You left the resort without telling anyone, without telling *me*. I thought you'd gone *sky-diving!*'

She started to laugh, then stopped. 'Wait, seriously? Why on earth would I? Anyway, I texted you to tell you that I didn't think Selena Hamilton should be on her own. I think she might have taken something. Luckily, I eventually managed to talk her out of sky-diving—'

'I didn't receive a text and you seem to be missing the point here.'

'Which is what, exactly? That I have to report my every move to you now? Well, you'll be happy to know that, aside from talking his wife down from a possibly fatal jump, I warned Roger Hamilton that if his eyes strayed to my cleavage one more time I'd gouge them out. I was very diplomatic about it, of course.' She smiled sweetly. 'Was there anything else you wanted to know?'

Ari couldn't believe his ears. He'd been scared out of his wits. And she was giving him sass. 'Are you serious?'

He watched her walk towards him until he could smell her. He raked a hand through his hair as she tilted her head and regarded him with steady eyes.

'Ari, you're seriously overreacting here. You can't molly-coddle me through this pregnancy. I know what this child means to you but I won't be wrapped up in cotton wool until the baby's born'

He whirled from her and paced to the window. 'You think I'm only concerned about the baby?'

'Come on, be honest—would you be this worked up if it was just me on that plane?'

The air drained out of him and he reeled from the accusation thrown at his feet. He opened his mouth but no words came out. Because the realisation that was dawning on him—had been dawning on him all week—felt too overwhelming to make sense of.

'Perla…'

'You know what I was thinking when I was on the bus?'

Slowly, he shook his head.

'I started off thinking perhaps I should count my blessings. My first husband was physically and emotionally unavailable but I *could* graduate to a physically available but emotionally unavailable one. And maybe, if this one doesn't work out, I might strike it lucky third time round—'

'There won't be a next time. If you marry me, you'll be stuck with me for this lifetime and the next.'

'Let's not get ahead of ourselves here. What

I didn't say was that the thought of an emotion-ally unavailable husband would never work for me. Not now. I'm learning very fast that I'm an all-in kind of girl. So I'm not willing to risk my future happiness on a man who won't open up to me even a little.'

The emotion that slashed through him made his gut clench hard. He couldn't breathe. Could only remain still as she stared defiantly back at him, dared him to react to the gauntlet she'd thrown down.

He opened his mouth; no words came out.

He shook his head, damning himself for ten kinds of a fool when pain rolled over her face.

'Or you could just get lucky. Since you're so determined to hammer home just how incompe-tent I am at taking care of myself, maybe I'll just die and save you the trouble.'

Perla heard the words tumble from her lips and felt shock bolt through her.

Ari's face whitened and he actually stumbled back a few steps. Horror gripped her at how cal-lous she'd been.

'Oh, God, I'm sorry.' She rushed to him but he flung out his hand to stave her off. 'Arion, I didn't mean it.'

His hand slowly lowered and he stared at her as if she was a monster. Perla's insides shredded as he took another step back.

'I'm sorry,' she repeated. Her stomach went into free fall when he remained silent. 'Please, say something.'

'Get out.'

'No, Ari. Please—'

He jerked forward and caught her to him. The kiss he delivered was harsh and pain-filled and devastatingly breathtaking. But it lasted less than ten seconds before he pushed her away and strode from the room.

She refused to shed another tear even though her throat thickened painfully with the need for release.

Going to her bedroom, she sank onto the bed, tried to make sense of what had just happened.

Pain had made her lash out in the worst possible way and strike Ari where it'd hurt the most. She'd gone too far. She had to fix it.

She rose, smoothed her hand down her dress and left her room.

He was in his study, his shoulders rigid, fists clenched as he stared at the ocean.

'Ari, we need to talk.'

He stiffened but didn't turn around. Grateful for not being thrown out, she stepped further into the room.

'We've both been through a lot. And our past is always going to be there. You were taking care of me the only way you knew how. I shouldn't have said what I said.'

He remained silent for a full minute. Then he turned. 'You want to know about my past? About Sofia?'

Heart in her throat, she nodded.

'My father fought for years to stay out of jail. He used lawyers and manipulated the system to try to escape justice. But the authorities were equally determined. The economy was in the toilet and he'd been lining his pockets with ill-gotten gains. They were slavering to make an example of him. Just when I thought it was ending, some other charge would be added to the list and the circus would begin all over again. The only people who mattered were my brothers and my mother. But even I couldn't protect them from the cruelty of the media and their so-called friends. Watching them suffer made me hate my father even more. Then he was convicted. Finally, I thought I could get some closure for my family. Before we could take a breath, he was gone.'

Perla frowned. 'What do you mean, gone?'

'He died in jail months into his thirty-year sentence.'

'How?'

'He caught pneumonia and refused treatment.' He gave a sharp laugh. 'After the chaos he'd caused, he went out with barely a whimper.'

'And you felt cheated?'

'I felt more than cheated. I wanted to hunt him down in the afterlife and strangle him all over again. I went on a month-long bender. I was on a very fast downward spiral when I met Sofia.' His eyelids descended, veiling his expression. But she saw his hands form fists. 'She…saved me.'

Perla's breath stopped. 'Oh…'

When he looked up again, his eyes were the darkest green, shadowed with pain. 'She brought me back from the brink of rage and despair. And I rewarded her by ignoring all the danger signs.'

'Surely, she must have known the risks of getting pregnant if she had a weak heart?'

'She knew. But she was convinced she would survive it. She was an eternal optimist.'

'Ari, you can't keep blaming yourself for what happened to Sofia. You got her the medical care she needed and she made a choice. The outcome was unfortunate but—'

'I could've insisted. I could've—'

'Ordered her about, just like you're trying to do to me?'

Colour slashed his cheeks and he looked away. 'You can't control everything, Ari. Sometimes you have to let go and let things play out.'

'Is that what you're suggesting I do with you? Let you run around until something unforgivable happens?'

'You're assuming that you're the only one who cares for the welfare of this baby. But I want this baby more than anything else.' It wasn't strictly true. There was *one* thing she wanted equally as badly. 'But in order to give this baby what it needs, we need to put the past behind us and move on or it'll keep tripping us up, dictating our lives.'

'Move on. Just like that?' he asked through gritted teeth.

'No, not just like that. It's hard, I know, but I'm willing to give it a try.'

'You're willing to try when you're pregnant with my child but can't even move on from wearing funeral black every day?'

Shocked, she stared down at her clothes. The idea that her all-black wardrobe was sending a particular message hadn't even crossed her mind.

'Moving on isn't as easy as you think, is it, Perla?' he queried in a soft voice lined with steel. 'Come and talk to me about moving on when you change the colour of your wardrobe.'

'I'm talking to you now. And I didn't choose this wardrobe. You gave me a little more than a day to join you in Miami when I started this job. The stylist knew my history and she assumed I'd want to be decked out in black all the time because I was a widow, and frankly I didn't think it mattered in the grand scheme of things.'

His jaw tightened. 'It mattered.'

'They're just clothes, Ari. The fact of the matter is I want love. I wanted it when I married Morgan and I want it now.'

His gaze lasered on her. 'Why did you stay married to him after you found out he was gay?'

Ice welled through her veins. 'He told me on our wedding night that he'd married me because he didn't want anyone to find out. Especially not his parents.'

'The ones you continue to look after?'

She gave a slight nod. 'They worshipped him but he knew they wouldn't accept his sexual orientation. And…he knew how much I cared for them. I'd told him about my childhood and the foster system and he…he told me I could still have a family, provided…'

'You kept his secret?' he finished harshly.

'Yes. I begged him to come out. I even fooled myself into thinking I was getting through to him last Christmas.'

Ari's gaze sharpened. 'How?'

'He told me he was thinking about telling his parents. That he just needed time to sort out a few things first. Now, I realise he was probably planning something else.'

'Something like what?'

She gave a jagged laugh. 'Oh, I don't know, maybe he was planning to emigrate to Timbuktu? Or New Zealand? He took a bribe to crash Sakis's tanker so, whatever it was, it must have been worth the risk to him.'

He walked slowly towards her until he stood in front of her. His eyes were still shadowed but the agony had lessened. 'He took advantage of your kind heart and your unfortunate past to prey on you. The bastard didn't deserve you. You know that, don't you?'

'I know but it doesn't mean the need I have has abated. It's still there, Ari. The need to be loved. But I know you can't give me that. Am I right?'

Hazel eyes darkened and he looked away.

She tried to ignore the sharp stab of pain in her heart and forced herself to continue. 'I told you I'd make a decision once we talked.'

He tensed. 'And have you?'

She ignored all the self-preservation signs and blurted, 'Yes, I'll marry you.'

His head snapped back. 'You will?'

She nodded. 'I can choose to live in a fantasy where I get everything I want delivered to me on a silver platter. Or I can live in the real world where I get the baby and the family I've always yearned for. Two out of three will have to be enough.'

He caught her chin and raised her head so he could look into her eyes. 'You will marry me. You're sure?' His eyes blazed with an intensity that drilled to her soul.

Nervously, she swallowed. 'I'm sure.'

He gave a single nod. 'I'll put the arrangements in place.' He headed towards the door.

'Ari?'

He looked over his shoulder.

'About…what I said earlier…'

He shook his head. 'Forget it. We have more

important things to deal with now.' He strode out of the room without another word.

Shaky legs carried her to the window as the tears she'd fought so hard against slid down her cheeks.

Against the stunning backdrop, the sun blazed down, uncaring that she'd given Ari the answer he'd been clamouring for, and yet she felt as if she was still slipping down a slope, destined for failure and heartache.

Her hand drifted over her stomach. For better or worse, she'd made the decision for her and her baby. She had to learn to live with it.

Three Pantelides jets flew out of Bermuda three days later, all headed for Greece and Ari's private island off the coast of Santorini.

Ari had announced that morning over breakfast that they were to be married in two days at his island home.

The news had been greeted with joy from Brianna but with more restraint from the two brothers. That neither of them looked surprised told her they'd been fully aware of the reason for Ari's mad dash to the sky-diving site yesterday.

Perla took the first opportunity to escape to the cabin bedroom. Ari was busy on the phone, presumably putting the arrangements he'd told her about in place.

The irony of it didn't escape her.

She was an events organiser who didn't even have a say in her own wedding. At this moment she didn't even know who would be attending; whether it would be a large ceremony or a hole in the wall with a priest and his brothers as witnesses.

She fell into a deep, disturbed sleep and woke to find Ari next to her. He was wide awake, staring down at her with a look on his face that stopped her breath.

Before she could speak, he cupped her face in his hands and slanted his mouth over hers. It was rough. It was deep. And her soul sang with the feverish joy of it. She was completely unprepared when he wrenched his lips away seconds later.

'Arion?'

In silence, he climbed out of bed and began to undress.

Perla watched him, mesmerised by the dark beauty of him and the stark need in his eyes that so echoed the one in her heart.

She shook as he came back and stretched out next to her. Naked, gloriously aroused, his eyes intent on hers.

'Do you really think we can move on from the past?' he grated out, his voice little more than a whisper.

An egg-sized lump wedged in her throat. 'We can work at it, give it everything we have. Brianna told me she didn't have a smooth childhood either.'

'She didn't.'

'And I don't think Sakis escaped your family's devastation but they seem incredibly happy now.'

He continued to stare at her, his eyes glinting with a sheen that made her heart twist for him.

She didn't utter a word when he reached for her, slid down the zip of the light grey dress she'd bought from the resort shop that morning, and pushed the straps off her shoulders. Her panties and bra came next. Then he untied her hair from its loose knot and spread it over his pillow.

He kissed her mouth, her neck, her breasts, all the way to the heart of her, each touch, each kiss making her tremble and moan, and fight back scalding tears.

With just his mouth he brought her to a shuddering climax, then kissed his way back up her body.

Then he tilted her head up to meet his gaze.

'What you said…about dying…take it back. Take it back now, Perla,' he commanded, his eyes dark with torment, his voice gruff with pain.

Her hand settled on his chest, felt his heart thunder unevenly beneath her touch. 'I take it back. I never should've said that.'

He entered her with a guttural groan that filled the room. With each thrust her heart filled with emotions she dare not let out, emotions she'd always dreamed of voicing to that one special person. The knowledge that they wouldn't be well-received made her bite her lip.

He hooked his arms under her knees and surged deeper inside.

Ecstasy mushroomed through her. 'Arion!'

The sound of his name on her lips seemed to shatter him. Caught in the vicious web of passion, he climaxed with a tormented groan, brutally ripped from his soul.

It took several minutes for their heartbeats to slow, for total silence to return to the cabin. But just when she thought he'd drifted off to sleep, he turned towards her.

'We may not love each other but I promise to take care of you, and to care for you. And I will guarantee you this. Every night. Every day. For the rest of our lives.'

Her heart lurched. Would that be enough?

It didn't matter. It was too late. Because she knew without a shadow of a doubt that she was in love with Arion Pantelides.

CHAPTER TWELVE

SANTORINI WAS JUST as magical as she remembered, even viewing it from onboard Ari's immense yacht moored half a mile away from the capital, Fira.

Far from thinking she would be spending the day before her wedding in Ari's villa, he'd brought her straight to his yacht once they'd landed.

Granted, the luxury that seemed an extension of the Pantelides name was everywhere her eyes touched.

But the feeling that she wasn't good enough to spend time in his family home refused to leave her. It didn't help that Brianna had been roped into keeping her company and was determined to cheer her up. It also didn't help that another stylist had turned up that morning with three full rails of brightly coloured designer clothes.

In a fit of anger and misery, Perla had sent the stylist away. She was perfectly well-equipped to choose her own clothes. Except now she refused to wear black or the grey dress she'd bought before they left Bermuda.

Leaving the suite that seemed to close in on her, she went along the wide galley and knocked on the door.

Brianna answered with a smile. 'I was just coming to find you. Oh, I thought you were getting dressed?' she said as she took in Perla's silk dressing gown.

'I was, but everything I have in my wardrobe is black. I was wondering whether I could borrow something from you?'

Brianna's smile widened, and she stepped back. 'Of course. Help yourself.' She waved her towards the walk-in closet. 'And shoes too, if you want. I think we're the same size.'

Perla gaped at the sheer number of clothes, her eyes widening as she spotted some seriously expensive labels.

'Yeah, it's something you're going to have to get used to. I sent my stylist away a few times in the beginning too. Then I realised I was just delaying the inevitable. Our lives are too busy to accommodate spur of the moment shopping trips, and things will only get worse time-wise once the babies are born, especially if you want to continue working.'

Perla bit her lip. 'I don't know what will happen. I don't know where we'll live or even if we'll live together. Because Ari has chosen not to discuss it with me.' Tears surged in her throat and she whirled away from Brianna's concerned stare. Blindly, she reached for the first thing that came to hand and pulled out a burnished orange slip dress. 'This one?'

Brianna nodded. 'It's the perfect thing to go shopping in.'

Perla froze. 'Shopping?'

'You're getting married tomorrow. The least you can do is invest in some knock-out lingerie that'll blow Ari's mind. A woman can't have too many weapons in her arsenal.'

'That depends on what she's fighting for,' Perla murmured. Dropping her dressing gown, she slipped the dress over her head. The cotton felt cool against her skin and the colour lifted her spirits a fraction.

'Don't give up so easily, Perla. You've come too far to stop now. If you want Ari, make him stand up and take notice. Sometimes it's the only way to win against strong-willed men.' Her expression held a determination Perla couldn't help but admire. 'Are you ready?'

With a last look in the mirror, she pursed her lips. 'Almost.' She dashed back to her room and dug through her handbag until she found it. Uncapping the scarlet lipstick she'd worn the night she met Ari, she boldly smoothed it over her lips.

Brianna was waiting for her on the deck. Her eyes widened, then her smile grew. '*Now*, you're definitely ready. Let's go.'

The shops weren't as sophisticated as those on the mainland but they provided an eclectic mix that satisfied her immediate needs.

Perla bought two sundresses, one yellow, one green, and a pair of low-heeled sandals. Against her protests, Brianna dragged her to a wedding shop with every intention of forcing her to buy lingerie.

But Perla froze as she spotted a dress on the hanger. The simple cream Greek goddess-style dress could pass for evening-wear or wedding dress. The front was plain and sleeveless and its halter neck design would keep her cool in the Santorini heat. But it was the back that took her breath away.

The lace pattern travelled down the middle of the back and held the skirt that hugged the hips and flared to the floor in a tiny train.

'Wow. With your hair caught up, that dress would look gorgeous on you. Provided, of course, you want to look fabulous for your wedding day,' Brianna teased.

Curbing her indecision, Perla bought the dress. 'Can we go now?'

'Just one more stop.' They went two doors away and entered the most unique shop Perla had ever seen. Scent candles in all shapes and colours stood on pedestals while incense burned from assorted sticks. 'Sakis calls this my *juju* shop. I tend to get my way a lot when I burn a few candles on certain nights.' She laughed.

Forcing a smile, Perla felt herself sinking deeper into misery.

Leaving Brianna to make her selection, she browsed the shop. As she made her way to the front, she met a woman in her early thirties. The hostile look she sent her stopped Perla in her tracks.

A torrent of Greek followed, to which Perla shook her head and shrugged.

Brianna turned sharply and frowned. The woman continued to speak, her voice growing louder.

'I'm sorry, I don't understand.'

Brianna rushed forward and grasped her hand. 'Come on, let's go.'

'What's she saying?'

Brianna shook her head. 'It doesn't matter.' She hurried out of the shop.

'Yes, it does. You know what she was saying.'

'My Greek isn't that great,' she said, but Perla caught her guilty look.

She came to a dead stop on the pavement. 'But you understood enough. Tell me, please.'

Brianna's lips pursed and a look of unease crossed her face. 'The whole island knows that Ari is getting married again. His wife, Sofia, was from a large family here in Santorini. I think that woman was her cousin. They know he's marrying a redhead and I guess she thought it was you.'

'Well, she was right. What exactly did she say?'

Brianna grimaced. 'I think she said... God, if I get this wrong and Ari finds out, not even Sakis can save me.'

Ice trailed up Perla's spine. 'What did she say?' she demanded.

'She said Ari and Sofia's love was a match made in heaven; the love of the century. She said...'

'What?'

'She said Ari will never love you the way he loved her.'

The sob that rose from her soul shattered her heart on its way up. She saw Brianna pale and reach for her hand but Perla shook her away. 'If I'd understood that was what she was saying, I could've saved her the trouble. I already know Ari doesn't love me. He never will.'

'You need to get over here, fast.'

Fear spiked through Ari at Sakis's tone. 'What's wrong? Is Perla okay?'

'Yes, she's fine physically but something happened when she went out with Brianna... Look, just get yourself over here, pronto, *ne?*'

Ari ended the call and glanced at the chaos all around him. Carpenters and decorators rushed to do his bidding, to set up the place for what most couples would deem the most important day of their lives.

But, deep down inside, he knew the most important day of his life had come and gone. The most important day of his life had happened when he'd thought he was too mired in guilt and grief to ever function properly.

Even when he'd looked up from his drink at Macdonald Hall and his world had shifted he'd refused to acknowledge the importance of it.

She's fine physically...

His breath shuddered out of him as he grabbed his jacket and ran for the door of his villa. Every day since he'd met Perla Lowell had been important but he'd been too damned afraid to admit it to himself.

Well, it was time to stop hiding and dare to be as brave as Perla had been. It was time to take care of the single most precious thing in his life *emotionally.*

He reached his yacht in record time. Sweat poured off his temples as he flew down the stairs, barely acknowledging Brianna's anxious look or Sakis ushering her away as he headed down the galley towards his suite.

He turned the doorknob and found it unyielding. He bit back a curse and swallowed down the fear climbing into his throat.

'Perla, open the door.'

'No.' Even through the closed door he heard the pain in her voice and his chest tightened.

'*Glikia mou*, open the door now. I'm not going anywhere until you do.'

'Go back to the island where you belong. There's nothing for you here.'

'You're wrong. Everything I want is right here. This is where I belong.'

The silence that greeted him tore at his insides. He leaned his forehead against the door and fought the urge to smash it in. 'Open the door, Perla. *Please.*'

Another minute went by, then he heard the scrape of the lock.

The moment it opened a crack, he slipped inside. The sight of her tear-ravaged face eviscerated him. He started to reach for her but she pulled away sharply. He clenched his fist to stop from grabbing for her. He didn't like the hollowness filling his soul.

'Tell me what happened today.' He'd already heard the gist of it from Sakis when he'd called from the car after leaving the villa.

'It doesn't matter what happened. I thought I could do it, Ari, but I can't.'

His heart plunged to the bottom of his feet. 'You can't do what?'

'Marry you. I thought I could but I can't.'

'Not even for the sake of our child?' He hated to play that card, but he was desperate.

The misery when she glanced up at him made his heart bleed.

'I thought I could but I will not come second best for anyone.'

He frowned. 'Second best? Who told you you were second best?'

'No one needed to. I have eyes and a brain. You brought me here and you stashed me on your boat. Out of sight, out of mind. The moment I ventured off the boat I was reminded why I'll never be good enough for you.'

'What the hell are you talking about?'

'Sofia, your wife, will always be the love of your life. The woman at the shop called it the love story of the century. I thought I could live with that, but I can't...'

He ventured forward and exhaled in relief when she didn't cringe away from him. More than anything he wanted to reach for her but he stopped himself. She could bolt, and that would destroy him.

'I loved her, I won't deny that. She saved me from a dark, bleak place and brought me back from the brink. But I wasn't the best husband to her that I could be. I failed to save her the way she'd saved me. I should've been stronger for her sake.'

'Every time you talk about her, I hear the pain in your voice.'

'Because, despite knowing that she had the best

medical care, a part of me still feels I let her down by not insisting she take the right advice.'

'So it's guilt that's been eating at you?'

'It was before, but not so much any more. As much as I regret what happened, I can't undo the past. You've taught me that I need to look to the future, to let go of things I can't change. And I have to believe that Sofia would want that for me too.'

'Then why did you stash me on the boat?' Her hurt was unmistakable.

'I'm sorry. I wanted to spare Sofia's relatives unnecessary pain, yes, but I also wanted to make sure the villa was ready for you. For our wedding. I haven't lived here for three years, and it was no-where near as ready as I wanted it to be.'

Her fingers twisted round the tissue in her hand and his heart twisted along with it. 'But why here? We could've married anywhere else in Greece.'

He frowned. 'You don't remember what you said to me when we met?'

Confusion marred her forehead. 'What I said?'

'At Macdonald Hall, you said your first trip to Greece was to Santorini. That you'd always dreamed you'd get married here.'

Realisation dawned and her eyes grew wide.

'Yes, *glikia mou*, I wanted to give you that wish.'

'Why?'

'Because your happiness means the world to me.'

She sucked in a breath. 'Please don't say that. Please don't make me hope.'

'Why not?'

'Because you'll make me want the impossible.'

'What do you want, Perla? Tell me what you want and you might be surprised by how motivated I am to give it to you.'

When she said nothing, he ventured closer. The orange sundress she wore made her golden-hued skin glow. Unable to resist, he reached out and took her hand in his.

The shiver that coursed through her echoed through him.

'Please tell me what you want, *agape mou*.'

Green eyes rose to his. In their depths he saw courage, determination, naked longing and another emotion he hoped to God was what he imagined it to be.

'I want you. To love me.'

'Only if you love me half as much as I love you, Perla *mou*.'

She gasped. 'What?'

He kissed her knuckles and closed his eyes for a second when her fingers trembled against his lips.

'I love you. I knew from the first that what I felt for you went beyond mere desire, but I fought it because…well, you know why.'

'But on the plane you said—'

'Something stupid about us not loving each other? That was pure self-protection speaking. I thought I could have what I wanted while protecting my heart.' He shook his head. 'The truth is, I don't need to protect my heart; not from you. Yes, what I feel scared the life out of me but what you and I have also fills me with joy even while making me a little crazy. Every time I look at you, I crave you. Every time I make love to you, I want to do it all over again, immediately. It makes me insane but it also makes me feel more alive than I have in the longest time. I never want to lose you because I intend to drive myself insane for a lifetime. If what I had with Sofia is being described as the love of the century then ours will be the love story of the millennia.'

Her eyes filled with tears he didn't hesitate to kiss away. 'Oh, Arion. I thought you were doing all this for the baby.'

'When I wasn't sure you'd take me as I was I admit I tried to use our baby to sway you.'

'And I let myself be swayed because I didn't see any other way to be with you. Now I can tell you that I love you too, without being scared it'll push you away. Tell me you love me again, Arion.' Her eyes shone with a brilliance that stopped his heart.

Happiness rushed into his chest and he had no problem uttering the words. 'I love you. I wish I'd admitted that to us both sooner. But I intend to make up for lost time. You have my promise on that.'

He kissed her for a long time, only raising his head when they ran out of air.

'The house is almost ready. But you have a free hand to change anything you want before the wedding tomorrow.'

She licked lips swollen from his kisses, making him groan. 'Um, can I practise a woman's right to change her mind? Blame it on all the pregnancy hormones rushing through my body right now.'

'What do you want to change?'

She touched his face, leaned forward until their foreheads touched. Ari knew he wouldn't like what was coming but he didn't care. 'The wedding date. The venue. The guest list. *Everything?*'

She stopped his groan of protest with her mouth. And he let her.

EPILOGUE

'Is this better?'

Perla placed her hand over her swollen stomach and sighed with happiness. 'Much better. I don't even miss the fact that I can't have champagne at my own wedding.' She glanced down at her hand and watched her new platinum wedding ring gleam in the setting Bermudan sun. The flash of her heart-shaped ruby engagement ring also caught the rays as Ari lifted her hand and kissed the back of it.

'You delayed us getting married for four months then refused to wait another two until the baby was here.'

'I thought I could hold out but the thought of calling you my own got too overwhelming.'

The look that crossed his face was one she'd seen on his brother's face as he gazed at Brianna. At that time she'd envied it. Right now, she basked in it and sent a prayer of thanks for her very own fantasy coming true.

'You've owned me since the moment I saw you,

wearing that lipstick you're henceforth banned
from ever wearing in public again. I just didn't
know it yet.'

'Better late than never, I guess.'

He laughed and they both turned when Sakis
and Brianna entered with their three-week-old
baby. Dimitri Pantelides was fast asleep in his father's arms, one fist curled around Sakis's fore-
finger.

Brianna arranged his blanket more snugly
around him, then looked up with a cheeky smile.
'Did you guys see the woman Theo came with?
She's stunning!'

'But she also looks as if this is the last place
she wants to be,' Sakis added, his tone displaying
a keen speculation that made Ari shake his head.

'And Theo the last person she wants to be seated
next to. The spark between them could've rivalled
last night's pre-wedding firework display.'

'Anyone know who she is?' Brianna asked.

Perla shook her head and looked at Ari, who
shrugged. 'He introduced her as Inez da Costa, a
business associate from Rio.'

'If she's a business associate, then I'm Santa's
Little Helper!' Sakis said.

Ari grinned. 'Think we should go jerk his chain
a little?'

'You stay here with your new wife. I'll go put
my son to bed and then I'll get right on it. I owe
him big for the ribbing he gave me during the

Pantelides Oil party on my island.' Sakis grinned with unabashed relish. He walked off and Brianna rolled her eyes and followed him.

Ari leaned down and kissed the side of Perla's neck. 'Before you think of leaving me because of my crazy brothers,' he said gruffly, 'let me tell you again how much I love you. How much I'm honoured to have you in my life and how much I adore you for giving me a chance at true happiness.'

Her heart soared, and she gasped as their baby kicked in approval.

'I love you too, Arion. You've given me the same chance too and there's nowhere else I'd rather be.'

* * * * *